In memory of my grandfather
Harry Joseph

Other books by
David Henry Wilson in Piper

Elephants Don't Sit on Cars
The Fastest Gun Alive
Getting Rich With Jeremy James
Beside the Sea with Jeremy James
How to Stop a Train with One Finger
Do Goldfish Play the Violin?
There's a Wolf in My Pudding
Yucky Ducky

Gander of the Yard

David Henry Wilson was born in London and educated at Dulwich College and Pembroke College, Cambridge. He lectures at the universities of Bristol and Konstanz, Germany, where he founded the student theatre. He and his wife live in Taunton, Somerset. His children's books have been translated into several languages and many of his plays have been produced in England and abroad, the best known being his comedy *Gas and Candles*.

Jonathan Allen is himself a writer with an original and bizarre sense of humour, as well as an exceptionally talented illustrator. When not writing or drawing, he plays bass guitar in a pop group. He lives in London.

Gan

of the

or Father Goose's Crimes

Piper Books · published by Pan

der Yard

by DAVID HENRY WILSON

drawings by Jonathan Allen

First published 1989 by J. M. Dent & Sons Ltd

This Piper edition published 1990 by
Pan Books Ltd, Cavaye Place, London SW10 9PG

9 8 7 6 5 4 3 2 1

© David Henry Wilson 1989

© Illustrations Jonathan Allen 1989

ISBN 0 330 31488 2

Printed in England by Clays Ltd, St Ives plc

"Gideon Gander is the Greatest Detective in the World."
Gideon Gander

And this must be the greatest detective book in the world, too. It contains ten of my most famous cases, including Death on the Farm, The Ghost, and The Missing Nose which almost gained me a knighthood – as well as nearly killing me.

I'm Gideon Gander, known as Gander of the Yard. The Yard belongs to Farmer Green, and that's where I live with my wife, Mother Goose, and our four goslings. Mother Goose sometimes helps me a little with my detecting (when she's not giving lessons to Gary Gosling, who is as much help as a pimple).

Farmer Green has a short temper, a funny way of talking, and a shotgun. Mrs Green is very Mrs-Greeny, and there are two Green children, Johnny and Bo-Peep.

You'll also meet Wolfie. I've been after him for years. If he commits half the crimes I think he does, he should be locked away for life. Or better still, for death. Wolfie is a master criminal, and one of these days I shall prove it.

Spiffy the Sparrow keeps popping in and out of the stories, too, but I can't decide whether he's a master criminal or not. I think he probably is, isn't and may be.

You'll also meet Tozer the Dozer, who is our watch-dog, Pussy and her kittens, and a lot of strange people including His Majesty the King. I don't like the King very much . . . (Mother Goose has just pointed out that the King might read this book.) I *do* like the King. I think the King is wonderful. Long Live His Majesty the King!

I hope you and the King will enjoy these stories. They are certainly the best detective stories that I have ever read – or written.

Contents

Lost Sheep

"Where are my sheep?" shouted Farmer Green.

"I don't know!" wept Little Bo-Beep.

"How did you lose them?" cried the angry farmer.

"I went to sleep," sobbed his naughty daughter.

"What, Bo-Peep, you went to sleep while guarding my sheep?"

"I didn't mean to."

"Well may you weep, Bo-Peep, if your sleep was so deep that you lost my sheep!"

"Yes, Daddy."

"Not to mention my rams and my lambs."

"No, Daddy."

"Oh, what a shock, to lose a whole flock!"

"Yes, Daddy."

"And sheep aren't cheap."

"No, Daddy."

"Well, you'll get a whack if they don't come back."

Little Bo-Peep sat waiting and weeping, weeping and waiting, but there was neither a baa nor a bleat to be heard. Very soon it would be whacking time unless someone could solve the mystery of the lost sheep.

"I'll take the case," I told her. "Don't weep, Bo-Peep. I'll get on their track, and when I find them, they'll come back with their tails behind them."

It sounded easy enough. Just find them and bring them back. The question was how? And where? And when? There were quite a lot of questions, really. And I couldn't answer any of them.

Little Bo-Peep told me all she knew. She'd been sitting under the oak tree, had fallen asleep, and woken up to find the sheep-field sheepless. The gate was wide open – though she knew she'd closed it. She'd run up the lane, down the lane and across the lane, but there had not been a leg of lamb or a woolly jumper in sight.

"There's only one thief," I said, "who's cunning enough to commit a crime like that. Wolfie!"

"Wolfie couldn't open a gate," said Mother Goose.

"Although of course ..." I said, pretending not to hear her, "Wolfie couldn't open a gate. So I think we'd better look at the scene of the crime."

Mother Goose decided that she'd bring the goslings along as well because they'd enjoy the walk.

"You can give Gary a lesson in direction-finding," she said.

Gary is our smallest gosling. He needs lessons in everything.

When we got to the sheep-field, we found the gate wide open. I'd secretly been hoping that we'd also find a flock of sheep, but no such luck. The sheep-field was as empty as Gary Gosling's head.

"No sheep here," I said. "But the gate's wide open."

It was a masterly summing-up of the situation.

Just then, Spiffy the Sparrow flew into the field.

" 'Allo, Giddy," he said. "Investigatin' a crime, are yer?"

I told him all about the missing flock of sheep.

"I shouldn't 'ave done it," he said.

"Done what?" I asked.

"It was me wot opened the gate," he said. "An' then I forced all them sheep ter run away."

"You did?" I cried in surprise.

"I get these urges sometimes," he said. "An' I can't stop meself."

"Well, there we are," I said to Little Bo-Peep. "We've found the thief. Now we just have to find the sheep."

"You opened the gate, did you, Spiffy?" asked Mother Goose.

"Yeh," said Spiffy. "Wiv me beak."

"Then close it again for us," said Mother Goose.

Spiffy looked at the gate, then looked at Mother Goose, and then looked at the gate again.

"A bit 'eavy, innit?" he said.

"No heavier than when you opened it," said Mother Goose.

"Ah!" said Spiffy.

He couldn't close the gate. And it seemed to me that if he couldn't close the gate, he couldn't have opened it. I told him so to his face.

"Please yerself," he said. "You won't get nobody else admittin' the crime."

Then he flew away. I had a feeling he'd been lying.

"I don't think Spiffy is the thief," I said to Mother Goose.

"You're the detective," she said.

And she was right.

I wasn't quite sure what to do next. Since the sheep weren't in the field, it was difficult to know where to look for them.

"Where exactly were you sitting?" I asked Little Bo-Peep.

Actually, I couldn't have cared two honks where she had been sitting, but I had to say something.

Little Bo-Peep showed me the exact spot beneath the oak tree, and I pretended to examine the grass. It was green. There wasn't much else I could say about it. The grass beneath the oak tree was exactly the same as the grass everywhere else in the field. But then I found something.

"Aha!" I said. "What's this?"

I didn't know what it was, but maybe somebody else would. It was small, pink and white, and sticky. And to my surprise Bo-Peep, when she saw it, went as white as a sheep.

"Let's have a look," said Mother Goose. "Hmm, it looks like the end of a stick of rock."

"Precisely," I said. What else could I say? If it looked like the end of a stick of rock, then that was what it looked like. But why had it made Bo-Peep turn pale?

"Now then, Bo-Peep," I said, "what is something that looks like the end of a stick of rock doing on the ground where you were sitting?"

"It . . . I . . . um . . ." she stammered. "I . . . I ate it."

"Aha!" I said. "So you ate a stick of rock."

"Yes," she said.

"Fair enough," I said. It wasn't a crime to eat a stick of rock.

"Who gave you the stick of rock?" asked Mother Goose.

The question seemed pretty pointless to me. A stick of rock is a stick of rock, whoever gives it. But then I saw that Bo-Peep was trembling all over and was starting to cry. It seemed to me that the question must be pretty important.

"Now then, Bo-Peep," I said quickly, "I want the truth. Who gave you the stick of rock?"

The answer was exactly what I would have expected if I'd thought of it.

"Wolfie!" she said.

"Aha!" I said. "Aha, aha!"

It was all beginning to take shape.

"It's my belief," I said, "that Wolfie gave you the stick of rock. Am I right?"

She nodded. I was right. And now that I was on the trail, nothing and no one could shake me off.

"And it's my belief," I said, giving her my most penetrating look, "that Wolfie stole the sheep."

"Yes!" she cried. "It's true. It's true!"

Then she broke down in floods of tears.

"There you are," I said to Mother Goose. "Didn't I tell you right from the start it was Wolfie?"

"You did, Gideon," she said. "You're a wonderful detective."

Once again she was right. On the other hand, I still didn't understand what the stick of rock had to do with it, or how Wolfie had opened the gate.

"Wolfie said he'd give me the stick of rock," confessed Bo-Peep, "if I promised to open the gate and then to eat the rock before I looked for the sheep. He said it would be a nice game. But by the time I'd finished the rock, they'd all gone and I couldn't find them."

"Aha!" I said. "So you opened the gate, ate the rock, and didn't look for the sheep till you'd finished the rock."

"I've just told you that," said Bo-Peep.

"I know you have," I said. "And I'm checking your story. It fits in perfectly with what I suspected. Wolfie is our thief."

I'd solved the mystery, but I still hadn't got the sheep back. And I had a feeling that Wolfie wouldn't be too keen to give them to us.

"The question now," I said, "is how we're going to get the sheep back."

"We'd better tell Farmer Green," said Mother Goose.

"Just what I was about to suggest," I said.

We all went back to the farm, and Bo-Peep told her father everything. Then he fetched his shotgun, and we all climbed on to his tractor and drove to Wolfie's.

Wolfie was lying in the shade of a bramble bush, licking his lips. He looked extremely fat, and obviously very pleased with himself.

"Well, hi there, Farmer Green," he said. "Nice of you to drop by."

"Where are my sheep, Wolfie, you creep?" asked Farmer Green.

"Sheep?" asked Wolfie. "What sheep?"

"*My* sheep," said Farmer Green. "Where are they?"

"No idea," said Wolfie. "Doesn't Little Bo-Peepy

here look after your sheep?"

"The game's up, Wolfie," I said. "She told us what happened."

"Well, it's my old friend Goosey . . ."

"Gander!" I said.

He always calls me Goosey, and that really annoys me.

"Goosey Gander," he said. "You're looking really juicy, Goosey. We should get together some time for dinner. My dinner."

I didn't like this habit he had of licking his lips. It gave me goose pimples.

"If you don't tell us where the sheep are," I said, "I shall have you shot."

"Oh, yeah!" said Wolfie. "And who's gonna shoot me?"

"I am," said Farmer Green, pulling his gun out of the back of the tractor.

"Hey, hey, steady on!" cried Wolfie. "Shooting me is against the law."

"So is stealing sheep," I said. "Where are they?"

"I know where they are," said Bo-Peep. "They're

behind those bushes.''

We all looked towards the bushes, and I could just make out some little splodges of white between the green.

''Sheep, sheep, call to Bo-Peep!'' shouted Bo-Peep.

''Baaaa-baaaa-baaaa!'' came the reply.

''Aha!'' I said. ''So you didn't know where they were, eh, Wolfie?''

Wolfie looked at me, looked at Farmer Green, looked at Farmer Green's shotgun, and then held up his right front paw and studied it.

''Er ... huh ... hmm ...'' he said. ''Sheep! Yeah, come to think of it, I did see some behind the bushes there. I didn't really take any notice of them. *Your* sheep, are they, Mr Green, sir?''

It was the moment I had long waited for. This time Wolfie was well and truly caught.

''We have a witness, Wolfie,'' I said. ''You gave Bo-Peep a stick of rock. Then she opened the gate and you took the sheep away. I am therefore arresting you for the theft of ...''

''Hold it, hold it,'' said Wolfie. ''You ain't arresting nobody. OK, I gave Weepy-Peepy here a stick of rock. I admit it. And that stick of rock makes the whole thing legal.''

"Legal?" I said.

"Legal," he said. "Listen. Supposing you laid an egg."

I'd beaten him already.

"Ganders don't lay eggs," I said, quick as a flash.

"All right, all right," he said. "Your wife lays an egg. Now I've got something you want."

"All I want from you, Wolfie," I said, "is your dead body."

I can be a pretty tough talker if I want to be. Especially when Farmer Green is there with his shotgun.

"OK, wise guy," said Wolfie. "So you want my dead body. Now supposing Dopey-Popey here *has* my dead body, and you want the body and she wants the egg. If you give her the egg, and she gives you the body, is that illegal?"

"Of course not," I said. "That's like buying you for an egg – not that you're even worth that."

I was winning this argument easily.

"Right," said Wolfie. "I wanted the sheep. Little Bo-Popeye wanted the stick of rock. So she got the rock, and I got the flock. Fair exchange, huh? Perfectly legal."

Maybe I wasn't winning the argument. In fact, maybe I was losing it. Then Farmer Green said that the sheep were his and not Bo-Peep's. It was a good point. Then Wolfie said that in that case Bo-Peep shouldn't have sold them to him, so it was her fault. That was an even better point.

In the end, Wolfie did give us the sheep back. But Farmer Green had to pay him for the stick of rock – and it turned out to have been the best quality rock, and very expensive. He's clever, that wolf. But one of these days I'll outsmart him. In fact, come to think

23

of it, I did outsmart him over the sheep. All but one of them, anyway. At least, I *think* I outsmarted him.

Death on the Farm

"Murder! Murder! They've killed my husband! Help! Murder!"

This was the cry that woke us all on a cold and frosty morning, and began one of the nastiest cases I ever had to work on. It was Mrs Robin who was crying, and when I went to see what had happened, I found her standing beside the body of poor Cock Robin. He was flat on his back, his legs in the air and an arrow through his heart.

"Who could have done it?" she wept. "And why would anyone kill poor Cocky?"

Those were precisely the questions I'd wanted to ask *her*. It wasn't a very promising start.

The next thing that happened was news of another crime. A loud *oink* from the pigsty was followed by the cry, "Ponky's gone!" There was a scream from Mrs Pig, and we all rushed across.

"Where's my Ponky?" she screeched. "Who's stolen Ponky? Ponky! Ponky! What have they done with my Ponky?"

No day had ever begun like this – and there was worse to follow, as you'll see later. Two crimes: murder and kidnapping. It was lucky there was a superdetective on the spot to solve these mysteries.

I began at once to question the witnesses. Mrs Robin had last seen Cocky when he'd left the nest in search of breakfast. He didn't return, so she came to look for him, and found him exactly as he was now. That was all she could tell me. It wasn't much.

Mrs Pig had last seen Ponky just before they'd all gone to sleep. He and the other piglets had snuggled up against her, she'd kissed each one of them goodnight, and when she woke up, Ponky had gone.

"Which piglet got the last kiss?" I asked.

There was no particular reason for asking the question. I just thought I ought to ask somebody something.

"Ponky," she said.

"Aha!" I said. There wasn't much else I *could* say.

I was baffled. But not for long. I quickly worked out that if a pig had been stolen, there must be a pig-thief around. And if there was a pig-thief, it could only be . . .

"Wolfie!" I cried. "Wolfie's the criminal!"

"Wolfie might steal a pig," said Mother Goose, "but he could never fire a bow and arrow."

That was true.

"Aha!" I said. "Then Wolfie stole the pig, and somebody else killed Cocky."

It was a clever theory.

At that moment, Spiffy the Sparrow flew into the yard.

"Wot's 'appened?" he asked.

I told him.

"Oh, well," he said, "I done that."

It was an amazing breakthrough. I'd solved the mystery.

"Aha!" I said. "I thought as much. Now, I want the whole story."

"Well," he said, "I shot Cocky wiv me bow 'n' arrer, didn't I?"

"I see."

"An' then I took Ponky off ter the market, didn't I?"

"I see."

"An' I sold 'im there, didn't I?"

"Then I shall have to arrest you," I said, "for murder and kidnapping."

"Wait a moment," said Mother Goose. "How did you carry Ponky to the market, Spiffy?"

"Ah!" he said. "Well, I carried 'im in me beak, didn't I?"

Now, I found that surprising. Spiffy is very tiny, and even though Ponky was only a piglet, he was at least twenty times as big as the sparrow.

"And how did you fire the bow and arrow?" asked Mother Goose.

"Ah!" said Spiffy. "Well, I . . . um . . . fired it wiv me beak, didn't I? Or . . . um . . . somefink."

I had a feeling Spiffy was lying. It's difficult to say why, but I have an instinct in these cases.

"He's lying," said Mother Goose.

"I know," I said. "I suspected him right from the start."

"What of?" asked Mother Goose.

"Being innocent," I replied.

"I confess!" cried Spiffy. "It wasn't me wot dunnit!"

Then he flew off to have a little weep in the gutter.

It was lucky that I'd spotted his mistakes. Otherwise I might have arrested him, and the real criminal or criminals would have got away free.

But if Spiffy hadn't done it, who had? I wandered across the yard to have another look at poor Cock Robin.

"Why should anyone kill my Cocky?" asked Mrs Robin again.

"I'll ask the questions, madam," I said. "Now then, why would anyone kill your Cocky?"

"I don't know," she said.

We were back where we'd started. I walked over to the pigsty and spoke to Mrs Pig.

"Why would anyone steal your Ponky?" I asked.

"I don't know," she said.

I was getting nowhere. If everyone refused to answer my questions I'd never be able to solve the mystery.

Well, if it wasn't Spiffy, it must have been Wolfie. It was time I had a word with him.

"I'm going to see what Wolfie had for breakfast," I told Mother Goose.

"Then be careful Wolfie doesn't have you for lunch," she replied.

I kissed her and the goslings goodbye. That took quite a while because I had to show Gary how to do it, but at last off I flew to Wolfie's.

"Hi there, Goosey!" called Wolfie as I flew over his head.

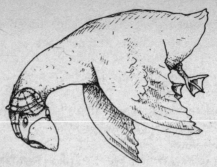

"Gander!" I said. I hate being called Goosey, but he does it just to annoy me.

"Then hi there, Gander Goosey," he said. "Nice of you to pay old Wolfie a visit."

"What have you done with Ponky?" I demanded.

"Ponky?" he asked, putting on his usual innocent look.

"Mrs Pig's Ponky," I said.

"I know she is," he said. "I can almost smell her from here."

It was no use asking Wolfie anything. I flew all round his clearing in the forest, but there was no sign at all of Ponky – or even bits of Ponky.

"I know you took him, Wolfie," I said. "Just tell me where he is."

"OK, OK," he said. "You just come down here next to me, and I'll tell you the whole story."

I didn't like the way he licked his lips.

"Tell me the story up here," I said.

"I can't get up there," he said. "Come down here and we'll have some lunch."

I remembered what my wife had said about Wolfie and lunch.

"I'm not that stupid," I told him.

"You could have fooled me," he said.

Talking to Wolfie was a waste of time. I told him I'd come back soon and arrest him for murder and kidnapping.

"Whenever you like, Goosey," he said. "And bring your lovely wife along, too. I've got room for both of you."

As soon as I came near the farm, I knew something was wrong. I could hear a bell going ding-dong, and Tozer the watchdog was barking. That was very unusual. Tozer usually spent all day and all night sleeping in the barn.

"It's Pussy!" Mother Goose told me as I landed. "She's been thrown in the well."

Cock Robin dead, Ponky kidnapped, and now Pussy in the well – this was a real crime wave.

We went across to the well, and I saw two pink legs waving in the air.

"It's Tommy Stout," said my wife. "He's trying to pull Pussy out."

Little Tommy Stout, son of the local piper, at last climbed out of the well, carrying the limp, wet body of Pussy. By now all the animals had gathered round the well.

"Pussy's dead!" someone cried. "Another murder! Who killed Pussy?"

"Tommy Stout killed Pussy!" cried someone else.

"No, I didn't!" shouted Tommy Stout. "I pulled her out."

"Then who threw her in?" I asked.

"Little Johnny Green!" he replied.

Just then, Farmer Green himself arrived, and I told him what had happened.

"Stop that bell," he ordered. "Now, if Pussy was in the well, maybe she just fell. Who can tell?"

But Mrs Robin and Mrs Pig said Tommy Stout had thrown Pussy in, and Tommy Stout said that Johnny Green had thrown Pussy in, so Farmer Green sent for his son.

"It wasn't me!" cried Johnny. "I've been looking after the sheep with Bo-Peep."

"You liar!" said Tommy.

"You murderer!" said Johnny.

I had a feeling that one of them was not telling the truth.

"Leave this to me," I said to Farmer Green. I could see the relief in his eyes. Such a case needed expert handling.

"Tommy," I said, "did you throw Pussy in the well?"

"No," said Tommy.

"Aha!" I said. "Then Johnny must have done it."

"No, I didn't," said Johnny.

Now that really was puzzling. If neither of them had done it, then who had? I was just wondering whether Wolfie might have got back to the farm before me, when suddenly the case took an unexpected turn. To everyone's amazement, Pussy gave a cough and a splutter and a miaow, stood up, and shook herself.

In a flash, I knew how to solve the mystery.

"Pussy," I asked, "who threw you in the well?"

Who else but a superdetective would have thought of such a question?

"It was Tommy Stout," said Pussy.

One simple question, one simple answer, and the case was over. But you have to know what question to ask. And when to ask it. And who to ask. That's the art of detection.

Tommy Stout tried to run away, but Farmer Green caught hold of him and held him fast.

"You don't get away from me as easily as that, Tommy Stout," I said. He knew he'd met his match in me. "Now then," I said, "tell us why you threw Pussy in the well."

"No," said Tommy.

It was an answer I hadn't expected. And it didn't help me very much.

"Why don't you ask Pussy?" suggested my wife.

It was a good idea. I wished I'd thought of it.

"Now then, Pussy," I said, "why did Tommy throw you in the well?"

"Because I saw him kill Cock Robin," said Pussy.

"Aha!" I said.

That was a real surprise. But with my usual speed of thought, I at once formed a theory.

"I think, Pussy," I said, "that Tommy Stout threw you in the well because he saw you kill Cock Robin. Am I right?"

"No," said Pussy. "I saw *him* kill Cock Robin."

"Aha!" I said. "Now we're getting somewhere."

"Why did Tommy pull you out again?" asked Mother Goose.

"Because we saw him!" cried Mrs Robin and Mrs Pig together.

"So he pretended he was saving me," said Pussy, "instead of killing me."

"What a dirty trick!" I said to Tommy.

"And why did you kill my poor Cocky?" cried Mrs Robin.

"Leave this to me, Mrs Robin," I said. "Tommy, tell us why you killed her poor Cocky."

"No," said Tommy.

That was the second time he'd said *no*. He wasn't being very helpful. But if he wouldn't tell me, who else could? I had a feeling I was losing control of the situation.

"Pussy," I said, "why did Tommy kill Cock Robin?"

"I don't know," said Pussy.

"But somebody must know!" I cried.

"I do," said Mother Goose.

This case was full of surprises.

"How can you know?" I asked. "You weren't there!"

"Look at Tommy's tummy," she said.

I looked at Tommy's tummy. It was rather fat, but otherwise there was nothing special about it.

"Unless I'm much mistaken," said Mother Goose, "there are several slices of Ponky in that tummy."

Little Tommy Stout went as pink as a pig's pimples.

"Cock Robin," Mother Goose went on, "saw Tommy steal Ponky, so Tommy shot Cocky with his bow and arrow. But Pussy saw Tommy kill Cocky, so when Tommy had taken Ponky home and had his bacon for breakfast, he came back here to kill Pussy, too."

This was all too complicated for me, but everyone else – including Farmer Green – was nodding as if they

agreed. And Tommy had gone as red as a robin's chest. All I had to do was find out whether Mother Goose's story was true. I did it in a clever but simple way.

"Tommy," I said, "is that true?"

"Yes," he said.

It was all I needed to know. Yet again I had asked the right question at the right moment.

Farmer Green gave Tommy a good beating, and Tom went howling down the street. Poor Mrs Robin and Mrs Pig were very upset at losing their loved ones, but they were grateful to me for solving the case. It remains one of the most horrible that I have ever investigated, and also one of the most difficult. In fact, I still haven't really understood it. But I have a feeling that Wolfie may well have had something to do with it.

The Bare Cupboard

Old Mother Hubbard lived with her dog in the cottage next to our farm, and one morning we heard a cry coming from her kitchen. I hurried over at once to see if I could make it my business, and thus became involved in a very strange case.

Mother Hubbard had gone to the cupboard to fetch a bone for her dog, but when she had opened the cupboard door, what had she found? Not only was there no bone – there was nothing at all. The whole cupboard was bare.

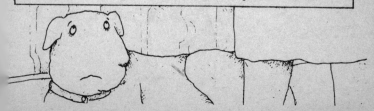

"I had three slices of bread in there!" she cried. "And a piece of cheese and a slice of bacon for my breakfast. And they've all gone! Who could have taken them?"

She was very upset, and so was her poor dog, who lay on the kitchen floor too weak and hungry even to move.

It didn't take me long to come up with a clever theory.

"I think you've had a thief in here," I said. "And I suspect the thief has stolen your food."

I was already halfway towards solving the case. Now all I needed to know was the name of the thief. It was time for me to start my questioning.

"Has anyone been in the house apart from you and Doggy?" I asked her.

"Yes," she said.

"Aha!" I said. "Who?"

"You," she said.

I thought about this for a moment, but there was no doubt in my mind that I was innocent. So I asked her another question.

"Has anyone been in the house apart from you and Doggy and me?"

"No," she said.

"Has anyone knocked at your door this morning?" I asked.

"Yes," she said.

"Aha!" I said. "Who?"

'You," she said.

It was the second time the finger had pointed at me. The evidence seemed to be building up against me.

"I didn't do it!" I cried.

"I didn't think you had," she said.

"Nor did I," I said.

But if I hadn't done it, who had? This case was proving trickier than I'd expected.

"I think someone broke in while we were asleep," said Mother Hubbard.

That was a possibility I hadn't thought of. It was worth pursuing.

"Think carefully, Mother Hubbard," I said. "Who would break in while you were asleep?"

She thought carefully.

"I don't know."

That didn't help much.

"All right," I said, "I'm going to look around the house to find out *where* he broke in."

At least that would give me something to do. I went to the kitchen door and examined it closely. It was open.

"Aha!" I said. "This is how he got in. Through this open door."

"I opened the door," said Mother Hubbard, "to let *you* in."

"But I didn't do it!" I cried again.

"I know you didn't," she said.

"Then stop accusing me!" I cried.

"I'm not accusing you," she said.

But she *was* accusing me. She kept saying that I was the one who'd been in the house, had knocked at the door, and come through the door. I was beginning to wish I'd never taken on the case in the first place.

"The thief couldn't have come through the door," she explained, "because the door was locked all night, until I opened it for you."

"Aha!" I said. "So the thief didn't come through the door."

"No," she said.

"But I did come through the door," I said. "So I'm not the thief."

"I know you're not," she said.

"Phew!" I said. "That's a relief."

We were getting somewhere at last. But if the thief hadn't come through the kitchen door, where had he come in? The front door turned out to be locked as well, and the windows downstairs and upstairs were all tightly closed. No house could have been less broken-into than Mother Hubbard's.

It was time for me to follow another line of inquiry.

"Food has been stolen," I said. "And I believe it's been stolen by a food-thief. And I think I know who that food-thief is."

"Who?" asked Mother Hubbard.

"Wolfie," I said. "I don't know how he did it, but do it he did. And I shall prove it. Somehow. I'm off to question Wolfie."

I left Mother Hubbard, kissed Mother Goose and the goslings goodbye (Gary had forgotten how to do it, so I gave him a quick lesson), and then off I flew to Wolfie's.

I got to the wood just as Wolfie was about to jump on a rabbit.

"Look out, bunny!" I called, and the rabbit dived down a hole a split second before Wolfie pounced.

"You nuisance goosance!" shouted Wolfie. "You've just robbed me of my breakfast!"

"You've already had your breakfast, Wolfie," I said. "You stole Mother Hubbard's bread and cheese and bacon, *and* poor Doggy's bone, and I can prove it."

"Then prove it," said Wolfie.

"Right," I said. "Mother Hubbard's food has been stolen by a thief. You're a thief. Therefore you stole Mother Hubbard's food."

I'd done a good job. Even Wolfie was impressed.

"I haven't been near Mother Hubbard's place," he said.

That wasn't much of an argument.

"Then how do you account for the fact that all her food is missing?" I asked.

He couldn't answer. I'd caught my thief all right.

"I'm arresting you," I said, "for the theft of Mother Hubbard's bread and cheese and bacon, and poor Doggy's bone."

"Hold on, hold on," said Wolfie, "you ain't arresting nobody, Goosey. How do you know Mother Hubbard's food is missing?"

"Because I've been to her house and seen the bare cupboard," I said.

"Right," said Wolfie. "You've been to the house, and you've been to the cupboard. I was nowhere near the house, and I was nowhere near the cupboard. So I guess that makes you the thief. Come down here, Goosey, and I'll arrest you for the theft of everything you wanted to arrest me for."

Why did everyone keep accusing *me* of the crime? I was getting really fed up with this, and I said so to Wolfie.

"It must be because you've got such a dishonest face," he said.

It was a nasty, hurtful thing to say, and it's quite untrue. I've got an honest and, in fact, rather handsome face. I've seen it many times in the duckpond.

I wasn't going to talk to Wolfie any longer if he was going to insult and upset me. I flew straight off without even saying goodbye. I hope that hurt his feelings as much as he'd hurt mine.

On the way home, I happened to meet Spiffy the Sparrow.

"'Ot on the trail, are yer, Giddy?" he asked.

I told him the story.

"Muvver 'Ubbard's place, eh?" he said. "Yeah, I flew in frough the winder an' 'ad a good ole binge, didn't I?"

"You mean *you* did it, Spiffy?" I asked.

"Course I dunnit," he said. "I masterminded the 'ole job."

"In that case," I said, "you'd better come back to the farm with me."

This was a slice of luck, and I didn't intend to let it go.

Before we went to Mother Hubbard's, though, I stopped for a quick chat with my wife. I had something very important to say to her. And what I said to her was this:

"I haven't got a dishonest face, have I?"

"No," she said.

It was exactly what I'd hoped she would say. Mother Goose is very intelligent, and when she says no, she means no.

I gave her a kiss, and told her that I'd solved the mystery of Mother Hubbard's missing food. Then she came with me to hear me explain it all to Mother Hubbard.

"Here we are, Mother Hubbard," I said. "Spiffy Sparrow is your thief. He flew in through the window, and ate all the food."

"But the windows were closed," said Mother Hubbard.

"I closed 'em when I'd gorn, didn't I?" said Spiffy.

"But I closed them last night before I went to bed," said Mother Hubbard. "Besides, how could you have taken Doggy's bone?"

"Ah!" said Spiffy. "I carried it away in me beak, didn't I?"

"It was a leg of lamb," said Mother Hubbard. "Five times your size. You'd have broken your jaw trying to get your beak round it."

I had a feeling there was something wrong with Spiffy's story. I sometimes get these feelings, and they're usually right.

"Spiffy's lying," said Mother Goose.

"Exactly!" I said. "And now perhaps we can get on with finding the real criminal."

Easier said than done. Now that I'd proved Spiffy was a liar, and with Wolfie refusing to confess, I'd run out of suspects. Unless it really was me, but that seemed very unlikely.

"It all sounds simple enough to me," said Mother Goose.

She's clever, but she doesn't know much about detective work. Any detective could have told her that detection is never simple.

"If the windows and doors were all locked," she said, "then the thief couldn't have come in."

"I know that," I said. "I've already proved that Spiffy didn't come in."

"Right," she said. "So if the thief didn't come in, he must have been in already."

"In already?" I said. "But I've searched the whole house. There's only Mother Hubbard and Doggy here."

"And you and me and Spiffy," said Mother Goose.

"Spiffy didn't do it," I said.

And then I had an awful thought:

"Good Heavens," I said, "you don't mean ... Mother Goose, my dear ... it wasn't ... it couldn't have been ... you?"

"No, of course it wasn't," she said. "And it wasn't you and it wasn't Mother Hubbard. So who was it?"

"Doggy!" I cried.

"Tell him to stand up, and let's see his tummy," she said.

"But he's too weak and hungry to stand up," I said. "Aren't you, Doggy?"

"Burp!" said Doggy.

"He's not too weak," said Mother Goose. "He's too full."

"Stand up this minute, Doggy," said Mother Hubbard, "or you'll feel a Hubbardy hand on your Doggedy bot."

Doggy stood up. Or at least his legs stood up. His tummy half stood up and half lay down.

"Aha!" I said. "So what's inside that tummy, eh?"

"Erm . . ." said Doggy, "er . . . ugh . . ."

"I know what's in there," I said. "You can't fool the superdetective. In there is bread, cheese, bacon and bone. Right?"

I was right. And Doggy knew he couldn't fool Gideon Gander. He confessed the whole crime. He'd smelt the bone during the night, opened the cupboard door, eaten all the food, and then pretended it had been stolen by a thief. And he'd have got away with it, too, if I hadn't come along to investigate.

Mother Hubbard was very grateful (not to Doggy, of course, but to me). Before I left, though, I had just one more question to ask her.

"Mother Hubbard," I asked, "what sort of a face would you say I had?"

She looked hard at me, thought for a moment, and then said, "A goosey face."

I'd have preferred it if she'd said a gandery face, but goosey was good enough.

"Would you say it was an *honest* goosey face?" I asked.

"Definitely," she said.

That proved it. Wolfie simply didn't know what he was talking about.

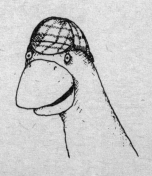

The Burglar

The Greens have always been afraid of burglars, and I don't blame them. How many burglars there are in our district I don't exactly know, but there is certainly one, and I suspect that he is the ringleader of all the others, if there are any others. His name is Wolfie. I shall catch him one of these days.

Whenever the Greens go out, they lock all the doors and windows, and although we do have a watchdog on the farm, I usually stand guard myself. Tozer is too old to tackle burglars. He spends all his time sleeping on the floor of the barn. A burglar would have to wake Tozer up and introduce himself before Tozer would let out a single woof. And even his woof would probably turn into a cough. But I am always on the alert, and can be relied on to deal with any burglar on four legs or two.

One morning Farmer Green, Mrs Green, Johnny and Bo-Peep drove away from the farm. Their car was loaded with luggage. I'd been asleep myself – even a superdetective occasionally needs his shut-eye – and so I only saw them as they disappeared out of the farm gate.

"Looks like they're off on holiday," I remarked to Mother Goose.

It was one of those swift deductions for which I am famous, and I waited for her to gasp in admiration and ask me how I knew.

"With all that luggage," she said, "they'd hardly be going shopping."

Of course she's learnt a lot from watching me at work.

It was a strange feeling to be left on the farm without the Greens. The thought occurred to me that if a burglar did come, there would be no one for me to warn. And I didn't much like the idea of tackling Wolfie if Farmer Green wasn't behind me with his shotgun. Fearless I may be, but I'm too clever to be *that* fearless.

Later that morning I happened to glance towards the house, and something caught my eye. There had been a movement behind one of the curtains. I didn't say anything to Mother Goose. I just looked the other way and hoped I'd been wrong.

I had to give Gary a flying lesson that morning. Gary is particularly bad at flying. Gary is particularly bad at everything, but he's especially particularly bad at flying. All you have to do is flap your wings and jump, but Gary can't flap and jump at the same time. So either he flaps and doesn't leave the ground, or he jumps and falls flat on his beak.

He'd just jumped and fallen for the tenth time, and as I glanced up in despair towards the heavens, I saw the unmistakable shape of a man standing behind an upstairs window.

Perhaps I should have kept quiet. But I was so fed up with explaining to Gary that you had to flap *and* jump, not flap *or* jump, that I actually welcomed this excuse for stopping. I went to fetch Mother Goose, but by the time she arrived, the man had disappeared.

"I think it's a burglar," I said. "I'm going to investigate, so could you take over Gary's flying lesson?"

Yes, I preferred tackling a burglar to giving Gary a flying lesson. That just shows you what a torture it is to teach Gary.

"Good luck, dear," said Mother Goose.

"And you," I said. She needed it more than I did.

I expected to find all the windows and doors locked, so that I couldn't enter the house. If I couldn't enter the house, I couldn't tackle the burglar. I felt quite confident as I approached the house, but when I walked round to the kitchen door, my heart jumped and flopped like a flying lesson. The door was open! How could the Greens have been so careless?

Now what was I to do? It might not be just one burglar in there – it could be a whole gaggle of them. With Wolfie, too, as their leader. If I went in, I might never come out again. Except inside Wolfie. I began to wish I was still teaching Gary.

The sensible thing to do was nothing. And so I stood quite still in the doorway, ready to race away at the first sign of burglary. But there was no sign of anything. Whoever was in there was keeping as still as I was. Maybe he was as scared as I was. Or maybe he'd already gone! Of course! He'd seen me from the bedroom window, seen that I'd seen him, and run downstairs and out of the kitchen door before I'd arrived. The house was empty!

I waited for a few moments more, listening carefully to the silence, and then I tip-toed into the kitchen. Not a sound. I tip-toed into the hall. Everything quiet. I peeped into the living room. Nothing. I peeped into the dining room. Nobody. I was doing a great job.

Now, whither should I wander? Well, I'd finished
wandering downstairs, and so I now wandered upstairs,
and strolled confidently into Mrs Green's chamber. And
what a shock I had. For there, kneeling beside Mrs
Green's bed, with his hands clasped together, was an old
man. And just as I entered the room, he said out loud:

"No, I won't pray! No, I won't!"

He stood up, turned round, and the two of us stood
face to face.

I don't know what he felt at that moment, but I do
know what I felt. Sheer panic. I was alone in the room
with a burglar, and not just an ordinary burglar, but
a thoroughly wicked one who had even refused to say
his prayers. It was him or me. Before I knew what
I was doing, I flew straight at him.

I gave his right leg a mighty peck, and he screamed. Then he ran out of the chamber, but I followed him, took him by the left leg, and threw him down the stairs. Well, I didn't exactly throw him, but I helped him on his way. Down he fell, bumpety-bumpety-bump, all the way to the bottom. And there he lay, groaning.

"You've broken my leg!" he groaned. "Oh, ah, you've broken my leg!"

"Good!" I said. "It serves you right for being a wicked old burglar!"

"I'm not a wicked old burglar!" he cried. "Go and get help, quickly!"

Then he made a sort of *oooeeeaaargh* noise, and fell asleep. It could have been a trick, so I gave him a peck on the nose, but he didn't move. This was my chance to go and get help.

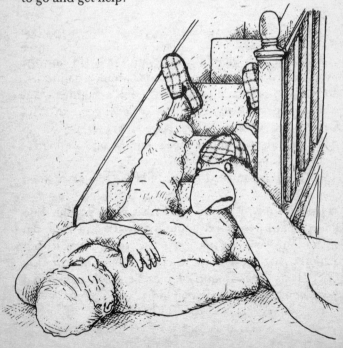

I hurried out of the house and into the yard. In the middle of it was a huge cloud of dust. Gary was now flapping and not jumping instead of jumping and not flapping.

"I've caught the burglar," I told Mother Goose. "Now I'm going to fetch the police."

"Good," she said. "Ask them to send the Flying Squad, and maybe they'll teach Gary."

I went to Mother Hubbard's cottage and knocked on her door. She was in the middle of her breakfast: three slices of bread with cheese and bacon. I quickly explained to her what had happened, and told her to send for the police.

"It's not the police you need," she said. "It's an ambulance."

Immediately she phoned for an ambulance, then put on her shawl and came hobbling out as fast as she could. Just before she closed the door, I caught sight of Doggy climbing on to the kitchen table and taking his first bite of bread and cheese.

"You must fetch the police as well!" I insisted.

"No, no," she said. "That's old Mr Riley, Mrs Green's father. He's come to look after the house while the Greens are away. Oh dear, I hope you haven't killed him."

I suddenly had a feeling that this case was not as straightforward as I'd thought it was. If the burglar was Mrs Green's father, then maybe he wasn't a burglar. But perhaps the man I'd attacked wasn't Mrs Green's father. Perhaps he was a burglar who'd killed Mrs Green's father and would have burgled the house if I hadn't attacked him. That was what I was hoping, anyway.

My hopes were dashed. The man at the bottom of the stairs wasn't a burglar who had killed Mrs Green's father. He was Mrs Green's father. And now he'd woken up and was groaning pitifully.

"I'm awfully sorry," I said. "There seems to have been a small mistake."

He stopped groaning when he saw me. He started screaming instead.

"Get that goose out of here!" he cried. "It's mad! Get it away!"

"Actually, I'm not a goose," I said. "I'm a gander."

"I'll wring its neck!" he cried.

"Now there's no need for violence," I said.

But Mother Hubbard shooed me out of the hall, and I saw her putting a cushion under his head and telling him to keep calm. At least she could see that he was being rather unreasonable. He may not have been a burglar, but he was certainly a wicked old man. What nice old man would refuse to say his prayers and would then threaten to wring Gideon Gander's neck?

At last the ambulance men came and took him away. He didn't even say goodbye.

Mother Hubbard telephoned the hotel where the Greens were staying, and they came back home that very same evening. I was pleased to see them, but for some reason they didn't seem very pleased to see me.

"Thanks to your beak our week's up the creek," said Farmer Green.

I thought that was a bit unfair. It wasn't my fault that Mrs Green's father wasn't a burglar. If it was anybody's fault, it was his.

"Perhaps you should have seen if he'd stolen anything before you attacked him," said my wife.

I couldn't think of a reply, so I didn't give her one. Instead I gave Gary a peck in the neck for flapping when he should have been jumping. It didn't help my case, but it made me feel better.

Mother Hubbard told the Greens that she would look after the house, and so once they were sure Mr Riley was going to be all right, they set off again with their car and their luggage.

There was one thing that still puzzled me. Why had Mr Riley refused to pray? Only somebody wicked like a burglar would kneel down and not say his prayers. I mentioned it to Mother Hubbard, and she promised to ask Mr Riley when she visited him in hospital. The answer she came back with made me feel pretty pleased with myself.

Soon after the Greens had gone away, Mr Riley had felt ill. He'd gone into Mrs Green's chamber to find some medicine, and had felt worse than ever. He then knelt down to pray that the Greens would come back to the house. But that was a selfish thing to do, and so he'd decided not to pray after all. And that was when I'd come on the scene.

"The funny thing is," said Mother Hubbard, "he didn't pray for them to come back, but thanks to you, they did. So you were the answer to the prayer he didn't pray."

I wouldn't say the Case of the Burglar was one of my greatest triumphs. But in the end it was a success, even if it wasn't quite the success I thought it was.

The Egg on the Wall

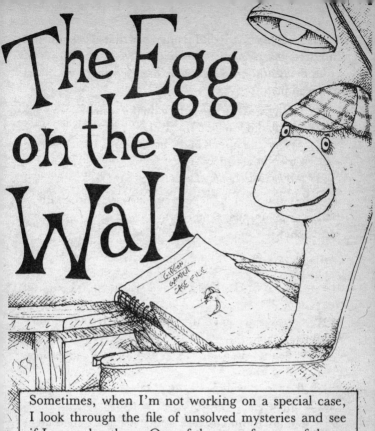

Sometimes, when I'm not working on a special case, I look through the file of unsolved mysteries and see if I can solve them. One of the most famous of these, which made me an intimate friend of the Royal Family – well, I spoke to the King, anyway – was the strange case of The Egg on the Wall.

The egg was known as Humpty Dumpty, and the facts written down in the file were as follows:

Humpty Dumpty did sit on a wall, did fall off the wall, and did smash to pieces. All the King's horses and all the King's men did try but did fail to mend the egg. It hath been buried in the courtyard of the Palace.

It was signed W. PITT, and was dated about two hundred years ago.

Underneath, in a different handwriting, was a list of questions:

(1) Why was the egg sitting on the wall?

(2) Why did it fall off the wall?

(3) Why did the King's horses and men *want* to mend the egg?

(4) *Who was Humpty Dumpty?*

The last question had been underlined three times. Beneath it, in the same scrawl, was the despairing sentence:

This case has me completely baffled!

It was signed S. HOLMES, and was dated about 100 years ago.

"I'm going to solve this mystery," I told Mother Goose.

"Oh, dear," she said, "I was hoping you'd give Gary a swimming lesson."

"It'll have to wait," I said. "The Humpty Dumpty case is urgent."

"I thought it was two hundred years old," she said.

"Exactly," I replied. "It's waited long enough."

I kissed Mother Goose and three of the goslings good-bye, and waved to Gary, who fell flat on his beak when he tried to wave back. And then off I flew to the Palace.

I landed in the courtyard, and started to look for Humpty Dumpty's grave. To my surprise, who should come walking along the path but the King himself. I knew it was the King because he had a crown on his head and was wearing a large badge that said KING.

"You're a goose, aren't you?" asked the King.

"No, Your Majesty," I replied, "I'm a gander."

"Funny," said the King. "You look just like a goose. What are you doing here?"

I told him.

"Good," said the King. "It's about time someone cracked the egg case. Come on, I'll show you the grave."

It was a very small grave, and had a little poem written on it: Humpty Dumpty sat on a wall etc. It didn't tell me anything I didn't know already. That was a pity. I'd hoped it might say why he'd sat on the wall, why he'd fallen off, who he was, and so on. That would have made it easier to answer S. Holmes's list of questions.

"I suppose you want to dig him up, then," said the King.

I didn't. I hate digging. But since there were no clues on the gravestone, perhaps it wasn't a bad idea.

"You really ought to get the Queen's permission first," said the King. "She's in charge of all the bad eggs. But she's busy at the moment, eating bread and jam in the parlour. Carry on, and if she makes a fuss, don't tell her I told you to carry on."

He said he had some work to do in the counting-house, but I had a feeling that he didn't want to help me with the digging. I myself sometimes pretend that I've got other work when Mother Goose asks me to do something I don't enjoy doing. Like giving Gary swimming lessons.

It was no fun digging up Humpty Dumpty's grave. Digging is no fun at the best of times, but there was two hundred years' worth of earth on that grave. By the time I got down to Humpty Dumpty, I was practically ready to join him. But at last I came to a wooden box with the letters 'H.D.' written on it. This could be the key to the mystery.

I opened the box, and found another box marked Hum Dum, which contained a third box marked Hump Dump, in which there was a fourth box saying Humpty Dumpty, which contained an egg-cup which contained a horrible smell. And under the horrible smell there were lots of pieces of egg-shell.

What was I supposed to do with them? If all the King's horses and all the King's men couldn't put them together, I certainly wasn't going to. The smell alone would make it impossible – I'd never be able to breathe long enough. The best place for those bits and pieces was in the ground, under a few hundred years' worth of earth.

I was about to throw them back in the grave when a ray of sunshine suddenly fell on the top piece and lit up a tiny mark. When I looked closer, I saw that it was the letter D.

"Aha!" I said.

Could this be my first clue? Carefully and with great courage (only a hero could have put his beak so close to that smell) I laid the pieces out on the ground and examined them under the sun. And by the time I'd finished examining them all, I had found the solution to the mystery. The letters spelt:

DNAECRIAMEFN

The only difficulty was that, although I had found the solution, I couldn't understand it. What was a dnaecriamefn? I hadn't the faintest idea.

Then at the bottom of the egg-cup I found another clue. It was a piece of egg-shell quite different from the others, hard and grey, and with the letters S. S. on it.

"How are you getting on?"

It was the King. Now that I'd done all the hard work, he'd come strolling up the path. He probably hadn't even been to the counting-house. He'd probably been watching me from behind a currant bush.

I showed him what I'd found.

"Dnaecriamefn," he said. "Obviously a name. Try jumbling up the letters and see what you get. As for that grey stuff, it looks like lead to me. I'd get on with the names if I were you. The Queen's good at anagrams, but she's busy at the moment, eating bread and fish-paste in the parlour. You'll have to do it yourself. I must get back to the counting-house."

Back to the currant bush, more like it. Or the parlour. I could have done with some bread and fish-paste myself. Breakfast seemed like two hundred years ago.

I worked on those letters for three hours, by which time my stomach was rumbling like a troop of King's horses. But I'd worked out the following list of names:

> Eric N. Deafman
> Damian Fencer
> Adrian McFeen
> Miranda Fence
> Dan Minerface
> Annie MacFred
> Fred MacAnnie

"Splendid!" said the King, wiping a shower of breadcrumbs off his moustache. "Now you'd better come along with me for a special treat."

Thank Heavens! I thought to myself. He's going to invite me to dinner.

No such luck. My special treat was a visit to the Royal Lavatory. At first I thought he must have heard my stomach rumbling, but it was not that sort of visit. All along the walls there were rolls and rolls of lavatory paper.

"Now then," said the King. "On every sheet of paper you'll find the name and particulars of people who've lived in this kingdom. If Eric N. Deafman and

Co. are anywhere, this is where they'll be. The Queen's good at this kind of search, but she's busy at the moment, eating bread and peanut-butter in the parlour. And I'm afraid I'm needed in the counting-house. Good luck!''

Off he went. I could guess what he was counting in his counting-house. Peanut-butter sandwiches.

By the time night fell, I'd scarcely finished my third roll of lavatory paper. Not a single sheet had mentioned Eric N. Deafman, Damian Fencer, Adrian McFeen or any of my other names.

"How's the roll call going?" asked the King, licking the peanut-butter off his moustache.

"Not very well, Your Majesty," I replied.

"You must be getting tired," he said.

"Tired and hungry, Your Majesty," I replied.

"Yes, I'm feeling pretty peckish myself," he said. "Anyway, I'm afraid the Queen wants to come in here now. The fish-paste and the peanut-butter, you know.

Come back tomorrow. I expect she'll be out by then.''

I scarcely had the strength to fly home. In fact I was so exhausted that I had to do a crash landing in the yard, and then crawl the rest of the way.

The goslings were all asleep. Gary had his eyes open – he hadn't learnt how to close them yet. But Mother Goose was still awake, and very relieved to see me.

"I thought you might be spending the night at the Palace," she said.

"There's no palace like home," I gasped, and fell fast asleep.

The next morning I told Mother Goose everything that had happened, and showed her my list of names.

"That's strange," she said. "Those names all have the same letters."

"I know," I said. "DNAECRIAMEFN."

"Well, you know what those letters spell, don't you?" she asked.

"Yes," I said. "Eric N. Deafman, Damian Fencer, Adrian McFeen . . ."

"No, no," she said, "those letters spell MADE IN FRANCE."

"MADE IN FRANCE!" I cried. "Ahem, well, yes, I saw that straight away, of course, but that can't be right because we're English."

66

"*We* are," said Mother Goose. "But maybe Humpty Dumpty wasn't."

Now, this gave me an idea. I wasn't sure about it, but it could be an important clue. I told Mother Goose what I was thinking.

"It's possible," I said, "just possible that maybe Humpty Dumpty might have been French."

I could see from her reaction that she was not opposed to the idea.

"But what would a French egg be doing on an English wall?" I asked.

"It could have been laid there," she said, "by a French hen."

"But why," I asked, "would a French hen lay an egg on an English wall?"

"England and France were always fighting each other in those days," she said. "The egg was probably meant to spy on the English army."

It was just a chance remark that she made, but suddenly I could see the whole thing. I'd worked out the solution! Humpty Dumpty had been laid on the Palace wall by a French hen, so that he could spy on the English army! I had answered S. Holmes's first question: why was the egg sitting on the wall? But could I now work out the answers to the other questions?

"I wonder why he fell off the wall," I mused.

"Where's the piece of lead that you found?" she asked.

I showed it to her.

"There's your answer," she said.

I looked at it, turned it over, turned it round, turned it sideways, lengthways, crossways, upside down, downside up . . .

"It's a pellet," she said.

"What's a pellet?" I asked.

"That's a pellet," she said.

"But what *is* a pellet?" I asked. (Mother Goose knows more words than I do.)

"It's like a bullet," she said. "It's fired from a gun."

"Aha!" I said. "But who would want to shoot a French egg?"

It was a good question.

"The English army," she said.

It was a good answer.

With a little help from my wife, I had now dealt with two of S. Holmes's questions. But the third one was tricky. If the King's horses and the King's men had shot Humpty Dumpty, why did they try to put him together again?

"They obviously didn't shoot him," said Mother Goose.

"But I thought you said they did!"

"I said the army did. But there's more to the army than the King's horses and the King's men. There's also . . . S. S."

"S. S. ?" I asked.

"The letters on the lead," she said.

"I know they're on the lead," I said. "But what do they mean?"

"Secret Service," she said. "Your Humpty Dumpty was shot by the Secret Service while he was spying for France. But the King's horses and the King's men didn't know he was a spy. They thought he was just an ordinary, decent English egg."

Of course! It was only natural for the King's horses and the King's men to want to mend the egg if they thought it was English. The questions that had baffled S. Holmes were no problem at all to G. Gander. And who was Humpty Dumpty (underlined three times)? Simple. Humpty Dumpty was . . .

"Well, who *was* Humpty Dumpty?" I asked.

"The egg on the wall," said Mother Goose.

I flew straight off to the Palace.

"I'm afraid you can't start searching yet," said the King. "She's still in there. Had a dreadful night . . ."

I told him that the search was over. The mystery was solved. And I gave him all the answers.

"A French spy, eh?" said the King when I'd finished. "And to think we had him buried here in the Palace courtyard. Well, Mr Goose, you'd better fill that grave in straight away, then take the gravestone and the egg and chuck 'em in the river. The Queen's quite good at chucking things, but she's busy at the moment, doing you know what. And I've got a pile of things to count

in the counting-house. But I'm sure you'll manage. Goodbye, and good luck.''

By the time I'd filled in the grave, and dragged Humpty Dumpty and his gravestone to the river, I was totally exhausted. Somehow I managed to get back to the farmyard, where I collapsed in a heap.

Mother Goose revived me with some water from the duckpond and a large helping of grass pie.

"Well, was the King pleased?" she asked. "Did he give you a reward?"

I told her what the King had made me do.

"That's not much of a reward," she said.

"No," I moaned. "You'd have thought he'd have given me a medal, or a peanut-butter sandwich. I can't understand it."

"Nor can I," she said. "But then, I'm not a super-detective like you."

Well, even if the King doesn't appreciate me, Mother Goose does.

The Ghost

It was Percy and Pamela Pigeon who told us about the ghost. They'd come to stay with us for a few days in order to get over the shock.

"We'd just settled down on the head of the Lord Mayor's statue . . ." said Percy.

"His right shoulder, actually," said Pamela.

"Oh! Well, anyway, the clock had just struck nine . . ." said Percy.

"Eight, actually," said Pamela.

"Eight, then," said Percy. "And this thing came out of King Street . . ."

"Queen Street, actually," said Pamela.

"What thing?" I asked. "What was it like?"

"It was horrible," said Percy. "Huge . . ."

"It wasn't huge," said Pamela.

"Well, not huge," said Percy, "but horrible. It was dressed completely in white. White, white, white. And it had these staring eyes . . ."

"Its eyes were closed, actually," said Pamela.

"Were they?" asked Percy.

"*Your* eyes were open," said Pamela. "And the ghost's eyes were closed."

"Well," said Percy, "it had these eyes that were closed but *looked* as if they were open. And it came right past us!"

"What did you do?" I asked.

"I did something on the Lord Mayor's head," said Percy.

"Right shoulder, actually," said Pamela.

It had obviously been a terrifying experience. Percy and Pamela had watched as the hideous creature had entered people's houses, knocking on doors and windows, and shrieking in a shrill, ghostly voice.

"I wonder if it really *is* a ghost," said Mother Goose.

"What do you mean?" I asked.

"It could be someone dressed up as a ghost," she said.

That hadn't occurred to me, but if it was true, then it was a case that I ought to investigate. If it wasn't true, I'd rather someone else investigated it. I've never yet met a ghost that wouldn't say boo to a goose.

"It's a real ghost all right," said Percy. "Probably someone who's just been murdered."

Now that was a clue, and it didn't take me long to come up with a name.

"You know who it is?" I asked.

"No," said Percy.

"It's Cock Robin," I said. "Tommy Stout murdered him in our yard . . ."

"The ghost is a hundred times bigger than Cock Robin," said Pamela.

"Aha!" I said. "Then I know who it is."

"Who?" they asked.

"It's Ponky the Pig. Tommy Stout murdered him, too . . ."

"It's not a pig ghost," said Pamela. "It's a human ghost."

Pamela wasn't being very helpful. I hate it when I build up all these brillant theories, and someone else just calmly sits there knocking them down.

"Well, what's *your* theory then, Mrs Brainy-Bird?" I asked, cleverly turning the tables.

"I haven't got one," she said.

"Then kindly leave mine alone until you have," I said.

Just then something very strange happened. A little white paper bag hopped through our front door.

"Boo!" it said.

"And boo to you, too," I said.

"I'm the ghost," said the bag. "An' I've come to 'aunt yer."

Now that was a surprise. Just a moment ago Pamela had told us the ghost was a hundred times bigger than Cock Robin, but this paper bag was almost exactly the same size as Cocky. So, had Pamela been lying?

"It's Spiffy," said Mother Goose. "What are you doing under that paper bag, Spiffy?"

Spiffy came out from under the paper bag.

"It was me all the time," he said.

"I'd never have guessed it," said Mother Goose.

"Are you investigatin' the case?" Spiffy asked me.

"Yes," I said.

"Well," said Spiffy, pointing to the paper bag, "that's 'ow I dunnit. I bin terrifyin' the 'ole town in me paper bag."

"Aha!" I said.

Then I turned to Pamela Pigeon.

"Yet you told me the ghost was a hundred times bigger than Cock Robin! But Spiffy here is the same size as Cock Robin. And furthermore, *he's not human*."

"And he's not the ghost," said Pamela.

"No, he's not," said Percy.

"Of course he's not," said Mother Goose.

I very quickly put this new information together, and turned to Spiffy.

"I don't believe you," I said. "Because I happen to know that the ghost is a hundred times bigger than you, and furthermore it's *human*."

Spiffy went very quiet. He knew he'd met his match.

But if the ghost wasn't Cock Robin, or Ponky, or Spiffy, then who was it? Percy suggested that I should go into town and watch for the ghost myself, but that seemed a bit dangerous to me. Instead, I came up with a new idea.

"If Mother Goose is right," I said, "and the ghost is someone dressed up as a ghost, then it must be someone who enjoys frightening people. Someone big, and bad, and nasty. And I think I know who it is."

"Who?" they all asked.

"Wolfie," I said.

"How can it be Wolfie?" asked Pamela Poke-her-beak-in Pigeon. "I told you, the ghost is human."

"Wolfie," I replied witheringly, "is a master criminal. He could disguise himself as anything."

"I'll bet 'e couldn't disguise 'isself as a sparrer," said Spiffy.

"You stay out of this, Spiffy," I said. "You've caused enough trouble."

I was determined to question Wolfie, although Mother Goose had in fact wanted me to give Gary a pecking lesson that morning. Anything was better than giving Gary a pecking lesson, which was one reason why I was determined to question Wolfie. I quickly said goodbye to everybody, and flew to the wood.

"Me a ghost, huh?" said Wolfie, as I circled over his head. "That's a howl. Why don't you come down here and tell Uncle Wolfie all about it?"

"No, thanks," I said. "If I did, you'd soon make a ghost of me."

I thought that was rather a clever reply.

"Yeah," he said. "Then my guest would be the ghost of a goose, I guess."

He'd got his facts wrong, of course.

"I'm not a goose," I said. "I'm a gander."

"And I'm not a ghost," said Wolfie. "I'm a wolf."

"You disguise yourself as a ghost," I said. "And you go through the town frightening people. That's what I think."

"Goosey," he said, "you don't think. You just make things up. Now you told me this ghost is human."

"Correction," I said. "It *looks* human."

"So it goes on two legs," he said.

"Or two hind legs," I said.

"And its head's at the top?"

"Yes."

"And it's dressed in white?"

"Yes."

"Then I'll tell you who it is."

I was a little surprised. Wolfie had never helped me before.

"Who?" I asked.

"You," he said.

That was an even bigger surprise. In fact it was a shock. How could anyone possibly accuse me of being a ghost?

"Goes on two legs," said Wolfie, "head at the top, and all dressed in white. The perfect description of you, Goosey. Ah, oh, help, save me from the ghost!"

Then he ran round the clearing, howling "HELP! IT'S A GHOST! HELP! HELP!"

Everyone would hear him. And they'd see me and think it was true. I flew away from that clearing as fast as my wings could carry me. When I looked back, I saw Wolfie lying flat on his back, kicking his legs in the air. I had a feeling that he was laughing, though *I* certainly couldn't see anything to laugh at.

I went straight home, and it took me a good hour to get over the shock of Wolfie's accusation. After that, I gave Gary a pecking lesson he'll never forget.

Percy and Pamela Pigeon were still staying with us, but meanwhile the Greens had given shelter to the first human refugee from the town. Johnny Green's friend William was a very pale boy, and I heard his mother telling Mrs Green that he'd been ill for the last few days.

"He hasn't been sleeping very well," she said, "so he might get better out here away from the town."

I wondered how many other little boys might be falling ill with fear like William. And how many pigeons like Percy, and pussies like Pussy, and dogs like ... well, no, if they were like Tozer, our watchdog, who slept all day and all night, they'd never see the ghost, would they? All the same, this ghost had to be stopped. I only wished I could think of some way of stopping it.

That night there was a full moon. There was also a wind, which made the timbers crack and the leaves rustle. Once an owl hooted, which was a very inconsiderate thing to do because it made me bump my head on the roof when I jumped. I simply couldn't sleep. I suppose I knew that something was going to happen. And it did.

The church clock was striking eight o'clock when out of the house and into the yard came a terrifying sight. It was human, dressed in white, and as ghostly and ghastly as a ghost can be.

I screamed at once. The others had to be warned, although to be honest I wasn't thinking of the others. I wasn't thinking of anything. I just screamed. Mother Goose and the goslings woke up, and so did Percy and Pamela Pigeon.

"It's the ghost!" they screamed, as if I didn't know.

Our screams woke all the other animals – all except Tozer, that is, nothing ever wakes him up – and soon there was a loud chorus of moos and bleats and oinks. But the ghost took no notice. It simply went round the house, knocked on one of the windows, and screeched something in a high-pitched shivery voice that made my neck-feathers stand on end.

Now, any normal gander would have been too frightened to notice anything else apart from the ghost, but I am no normal gander. What I had noticed was that while the rest of us were screaming, Mother Goose was not making a sound. She was just watching the ghost and occasionally nodding her head. Then suddenly she did something quite amazing. Instead of sensibly screaming and trembling like everybody else, she jumped out of our box and flew straight towards the hideous creature.

Its shrill voice was calling out some ghostly message – it sounded like 'all the children . . .' – when Mother Goose arrived and gave it a peck in the leg. The ghost let out a scream that was almost as loud as mine, and then . . . I could hardly believe my ears: it started to cry!

"Wah! Wah!" it cried. "I want my mummy!"

Farmer Green now came out of the house – he must have heard the screams, moos, bleats and oinks – and I saw that he had his shotgun in one hand and a torch in the other. He shone the torch on the ghost, and then I realized that it wasn't a ghost at all. It was Little William in his nightshirt. Farmer Green picked him up, gave him a pat and a cuddle, and carried him back into the house.

"Was that your ghost, then?" Mother Goose asked Percy and Pamela.

"We *thought* it was a ghost," said Percy.

"Well, actually," said Pamela, "I had a feeling it might be a little boy."

"Then why didn't you say so?" I asked. "You could have saved me a lot of trouble."

"Well, Percy said it was a ghost," she replied, "and I didn't like to contradict him."

There were still a few things that I hadn't understood. Why had the little boy pretended to be a ghost in the first place, and why did he go round frightening people?

I asked Mother Goose these very questions.

"He didn't," said Mother Goose. "He was just walking in his sleep. He only woke up when I pecked him in the leg."

It was the final piece in the puzzle. The following morning, when I'd fully recovered from the shocks of that night, I set to work putting the pieces together. William had gone to bed like any other boy, had fallen asleep, and then had got up, still asleep and still in his nightgown, left the house and run through the town. Percy and Pamela had seen him, and had thought he was a ghost. But he wasn't a ghost. He was William.

What had made him ill?

Mother Goose found the answer to that question.

"If he'd been running through the town all night," she said, "by the time he woke up in the morning, he must have been tired out."

The mystery had been completely solved. Yet another success for Gideon Gander of the Yard.

The next day William's parents came to fetch him. I heard Farmer Green explaining to them all about the sleep-walking, and they said they would take him to a sleepologist to get him cured.

Then they thanked Farmer and Mrs Green for finding out the cause of William's illness. They thanked them, and they didn't thank me! I'd done all the work, and other people took all the credit.

"I shouldn't worry about it," said Mother Goose. "It happens all the time."

But I was worried about it, and I waited by the farm gate to see William and his parents off. Just one thank you was all I wanted. But I never got it.

"Goodbye Farmer Green! Goodbye Mrs Green! Goodbye Johnny! Goodbye Bo-Peep! And thank you again!" they cried.

"Goodbye Mr and Mrs Winkie!" called the Greens. "And goodbye Wee Willie!"

Fiddlestick

It was the day of the Harvest Ball. This was the big occasion on Green's Farm, with people coming from miles around to celebrate the end of harvest. The ball was to be held in the barn, where there would be feasting and music and dancing all night long. For a whole week now, the Greens and their friends and helpers had been getting things ready, and in particular Farmer Green and Mrs Green had been practising. Farmer Green was famous for his fiddle-playing, and Mrs Green was equally famous for her dancing, and the highlight of the ball would be when the two of them performed together.

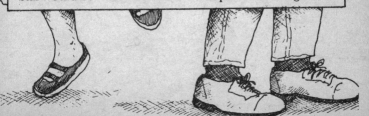

It was a lovely, sunny morning, and the barn looked beautiful with all its decorations. The only thing in the barn that wasn't beautiful was old Tozer the watchdog, who was asleep, as usual, in the corner.

"The perfect day for the ball," I said to Mother Goose.

"Yes, indeed," she said. "And the perfect morning for Gary to have his dancing lesson."

I'd forgotten about Gary's dancing lesson. I wished Mother Goose had forgotten about it, too. Gary is hopeless at dancing. Gary is hopeless at everything. If you tell him to move his left foot, he flaps his right wing; if you tell him to move his right foot, he waggles his tail; and if you tell him to move both feet, he falls over.

I explained this to Mother Goose.

"Then tell him to flap his right wing," she said.

"What's the good of that?" I asked.

"Because then he'll move his left foot," she said. "And if you tell him to waggle his tail, he'll move his right foot. It's quite simple."

Nothing is ever simple with Gary. Do you know what he did when I told him to flap his right wing? He flapped his right wing.

"Cock a doodle doo!"

I stopped the lesson immediately.

"Cock a doodle doo!"

"Did you hear that?" I called to Mother Goose.

"It's only Doodle," she said.

I knew it was Doodle. You didn't have to be a super-detective to know it was Doodle. But it was also an excuse to stop the lesson.

"That's very strange," I said. "That's very, very strange."

"What is?" asked Mother Goose.

"That Doodle should be crowing at *this* time of day."

Well, it wasn't all that strange. Doodle could crow at any time of the day that suited him. But why was he crowing at this particular moment?

"I think I'd better find out what's wrong," I said. "Perhaps, dear, you could just take over Gary's dancing lesson while I'm gone."

I hurried away to see Doodle. And to my surprise, there *was* something wrong – something very wrong indeed.

"Mrs Green's lost her shoe," said Doodle, "and Farmer Green's lost his fiddlestick."

This was bad news. Without her shoe, Mrs Green wouldn't be able to dance, and without his fiddlestick, Farmer Green wouldn't be able to fiddle.

I hurried to the house. Mrs Green was in tears, and Farmer Green was tearing out what was left of his hair.

"What a wicked trick to nick my stick!" stormed Farmer Green.

"And my shoe, too!" wept Mrs Green.

I asked them what had happened, and their reply confirmed the theory that I had already formed: Mrs Green had lost her shoe, and Farmer Green had lost his fiddlestick. In a flash I knew what to do.

"They must be found!" I said.

I could see the gratitude in their eyes. They knew that Gideon Gander had already decided to take on the case.

First I needed to know where the articles had been taken from.

"The stick," said Farmer Green, "was with the fiddle in the middle of the hey diddle diddle."

But only the stick had been taken. The fiddle was still there.

"And my shoe was in the loo," said Mrs Green.

But only her left shoe had been taken. Her right shoe was still there.

Now, who would take a stick without a fiddle and a left shoe without a right shoe? I needed an answer to this question.

"Think carefully," I said to Mrs Green. "Who could have taken your shoe?"

"We haven't a clue who took the shoe," snapped Farmer Green. "And if we knew we could do without you."

It wasn't a very helpful remark.

"I don't know," wept Mrs Green. "My left shoe wouldn't be of any use to anyone."

"Except," I said, with a flash of sheer genius, "to a one-legged woman."

They hadn't thought of that, though Farmer Green suggested it would be easier for such a woman to hop to a proper shop.

"You're forgetting," I said, "that she also took the fiddlestick."

And this could mean only one thing. Our thief was a one-legged woman fiddler. It was a superb piece of reasoning, and it narrowed the field considerably. All Farmer Green had to do was phone the woman fiddlers listed in the telephone book and ask them how many legs they had. But he refused to do it.

"No thanks," he said. "With such a prank I'd rank as a crank."

But Mrs Green agreed to telephone the Musicians' Union. After all, she said, there couldn't be *that* many one-legged woman fiddlers.

It turned out there weren't *any* one-legged woman fiddlers. So now I needed to find a new solution. It didn't take me long. Whoever had stolen the shoe and the stick would ruin the Harvest Ball. Who, then, would want to ruin the Harvest Ball? It could only be a thief with a nasty, cruel, selfish nature. A thief who enjoyed spoiling other people's pleasure. And one name sprang to mind immediately. Wolfie! It would be just like Wolfie to disguise himself as a one-legged woman fiddler, so that he could come and spoil everyone else's fun.

I left the Greens and went to tell Mother Goose what had happened. When I arrived, she was just trying to untangle Gary's left wing from underneath his left leg.

"Ready for the ball, is he?" I asked.

"Yes," she said. "The cannonball. You can take over now."

"I'm terribly sorry," I said, "I really am, but unfortunately I haven't got time. And I'd really been looking forward to giving Gary his dancing lesson."

Then I told her the whole story.

"So I've got to go to Wolfie's," I said, "to fetch the shoe and fiddlestick."

"No need," said a familiar voice. "Forget about Wolfie. I'm the one wot's got 'em."

It was Spiffy the Sparrow.

"You, Spiffy?" I asked in surprise.

"Yeh," he said. "I lifted the left shoe, an' I stole the stick."

"But why?" I asked.

"'Cos I'm wicked," he said. "An' I'm a master criminal."

"What did you do with the shoe?" asked Mother Goose.

"I weared it, didn't I?" replied Spiffy.

"And what did you do with the fiddlestick?" she asked.

"Ah!" said Spiffy. "Well, I did wot ev'rybody does wiv a fiddlestick, didn't I?"

"And what's that?" asked Mother Goose.

"Erm ... well ... I ... um ... I sticked a fiddle wiv it, didn't I?"

"Sticked a fiddle?" I asked. (I'd never heard that expression before.)

"Yeh," he said. "Mended it, like. Sticked it tergevver."

"A fiddlestick," said Mother Goose, "is a bow, not a tube of glue."

"I know that," said Spiffy. "Arter I'd mended the fiddle, I put the fiddlestick in me 'air."

"You haven't got any hair!" I cried.

He was lying. How could he have put the fiddlestick in his hair when he hadn't got any hair? I'd caught him out good and proper.

"A fiddlestick is a violin bow," said Mother Goose, "not a hair bow."

Spiffy looked at her, looked at me, then looked at his feet.

"No one never believes me," he said sadly.

"You need to be a lot cleverer than that, Spiffy," I said, "if you want to deceive Gideon Gander."

It was time for me to fly off to Wolfie's, but I didn't go. What stopped me was a suggestion from Mother Goose.

"If the thief only took Mrs Green's left shoe," she said, "why don't you get Tozer to smell the right one and then follow the scent?"

Here, I must give myself credit where credit is due. I do recognize a good idea when I hear it. I realized immediately that this could be a way of finding Mrs Green's left shoe. It could even lead to Farmer Green's fiddlestick.

I went straight to the house and explained our idea to Farmer and Mrs Green. They were very impressed and came with me to the barn, where Tozer was fast asleep, as usual, in his corner.

"Wake up, Tozer!" I said.

He gave a loud snore.

"Wake up, Tozer you dozer!" snapped Farmer Green, and gave the old dog a shake. Tozer wearily opened one eye.

I held Mrs Green's right shoe under his nose.

"Phew!" said Tozer.

"Follow the scent!" I said. "Good boy, Tozer, follow the scent!"

He didn't move. "What for?" he asked.

I explained what had happened.

"I'm too tired," he yawned. "*You* follow the scent."

"Tozer, you lump," snapped Farmer Green, "if you don't jump you'll get a thump on the rump."

Farmer Green is not a man to argue with, and even

Tozer jumps when Farmer Green tells him to jump.
But this time he didn't. He refused even to stand up.
He simply lay there, glaring and growling.

"On the track, you great sack!" shouted Farmer
Green, and gave him a cracking smack on the backside.

But still Tozer wouldn't move, and so Farmer Green
seized him by the collar and dragged him out of the
corner like a bag of potatoes. Then all was revealed.
For, lying in the corner, in the very spot that Tozer
had refused to leave, were one left shoe and one fiddlestick.

"Aha!" I cried. "What's this?"

"What does it look like?" growled Tozer.

"It looks like one left shoe and one fiddlestick!" I
cried.

"Ugh! Brilliant!" growled Tozer.

"Mrs Green, I think this is your left shoe," I said.
"And Farmer Green, it's my belief that this is your
fiddlestick."

"It's true! It's my shoe!" cried Mrs Green. "Well
done, Gideon!"

"He's done the trick! That's my stick!" cried Farmer
Green. "Congratulations on your investigations!"

I have never seen my dame and my master so happy, and I was proud to think that it was my very own super-powers of detection that had saved the Harvest Ball. But the case was not quite finished. I still had one more question left for Tozer.

"Now then, Tozer," I said, "why did you do it?"

He knew he was beaten. Once Gideon Gander is on the trail, he never gives up. It just took one more slap from Farmer Green to bring forth the answer. It was quite simple. Tozer always sleeps in the barn, and the barn was to be used for the Harvest Ball. The only way Tozer could have his sleep in peace was to stop the Harvest Ball, and the only way he could do this was by stopping Mrs Green from dancing and Farmer Green from fiddling. It was a clever plan. But it wasn't clever enough to fool Gideon Gander.

Mittens

"We've lost our mittens! Uncle Gideon, Uncle Gideon, mee-ow, mee-ow! Please help us to find them, or Mummy won't give us any pie!"

The three little kittens were very upset. Pussy (now fully recovered from her spell in the well) had given them all mittens to keep their little paws warm, and now the mittens had gone. There was only one way they could get them back: ask Uncle Gideon.

"Calm down, kittens," I said. "Calm down and tell me what happened."

"I took my mittens off when I went to bed," said the first kitten, "and when I woke up, they were gone."

"So were mine," said the second kitten.

"Mine, too," said the third kitten.

"Where was your mummy when you woke up?" I asked.

"She was chasing mice in Farmer Green's barn," said the first kitten.

"Then she came back," said the second kitten.

"And we told her our mittens were missing, and she said we couldn't have any pie!" wailed the third kitten.

They all started crying pitifully, because for a kitten not to have any pie is a terrible punishment. I could see at once that the kittens wanted their mittens to be found, but first they would have to answer two simple questions: (1) Who had taken the mittens? (2) Where were they?

"Who took the mittens?" I asked.

"We don't know!" they cried.

"Where *are* the mittens?" I asked.

"We don't know!" they cried again.

It was a bad start to the case.

I needed to know exactly how many mittens were missing. There were three kittens, and each had four feet, but . . .

"How many mittens are missing?" I asked.

"Twelve," said the third kitten.

That saved me a bit of time. Arithmetic is not my strong subject. Now I knew that twelve mittens were missing, and since the kittens couldn't tell me who had taken them, it was up to me to guess the name of the thief. Well, what sort of thief would enjoy stealing kittens' mittens, getting them into trouble, and making sure they didn't get any pie? One name stood out above all others: Wolfie.

But when I mentioned this to Mother Goose, she shook her head.

"If Wolfie had stolen the mittens," she said, "he'd have stolen the kittens as well, and gobbled them up for breakfast."

The kittens all shuddered and said: "Who me? Ow me! Mee-ow!"

Just then, Spiffy the Sparrow flew into the yard.

"Whassa trouble?" he asked.

I told him about the kittens' mittens.

"Oh, them!" he said. "Yeh, well, it was me wot took 'em, wasn't it?"

"You, Spiffy?" I asked. "But what use are mittens to you?"

"They keeps the nest nice 'n' warm, don't they?"

I'd caught him out straight away this time. Mittens are for wearing on the feet, not putting in a nest. I told him so.

"I'm fed up wiv you lot," said Spiffy. "Yer never believe wot I tell yer, so I don't know why I bovver!"

Off he flew, leaving me free to find the real thief. But there wasn't much for me to go on. My only clue was that there were twelve mittens. That meant twelve feet.

"It seems to me," I said, "that we're looking for a thief with twelve feet. There can't be many of those around. Unless . . ." I suddenly had a flash of arithmetic: ". . . It could have been two six-footed thieves!"

"It might have been four three-footed thieves," said the first kitten.

"Or six two-footed thieves," said the second.

"Or it might," said the third kitten, "it might . . . mee-ow . . . have been twelve one-legged thieves."

They all giggled. I reminded them that if I didn't find the thief or thieves and the mittens, they wouldn't get any pie. That soon shut them up.

At that moment we heard some loud noises coming from the barn: MIAOWSSSSMIAOW! WOOFGRRRRWOOF! SSSSMIAOWSSSS! GRRRRWOOFGRRRR! We all hurried across and found Pussy standing in front of Tozer, who was lying in his usual corner. It didn't take me long to work out that the MIAOWSSSS noises were coming from Pussy, and the GRRRRWOOF noises from Tozer.

"Aha!" I said. "So we've found our thief!"

"Go away!" growled Tozer.

"Move yoursssself!" hissed Pussy.

"I won't," growled Tozer.

"You musssst!" hissed Pussy.

"Leave this to me," I said. "Where are they?"

"Where are what?" asked Pussy.

"What are where?" asked Tozer.

"The mittens," I said. "Come on, Tozer, get up and let us have them."

"What mittens?" he asked.

"The kittens' mittens," I said.

"Don't know anything about mittens," moaned Tozer. "All I want is a bit of sleep."

"The kittens must find their own mittens," said Pussy. "They lost them, so they must find them. And if they don't, they won't get any pie."

The kittens began to cry again, and I began to feel a little confused. If Pussy had found the mittens underneath Tozer, why was she now telling the kittens to find them? It didn't make sense.

"If that mouse is hiding behind you, Tozer," said Pussy, "I shall tell Farmer Green, and then you'll see what you'll get."

"Aha!" I said.

I had suddenly had an idea which might clear up this particular mystery.

"I've got a feeling," I said to Pussy, "that you were chasing a mouse. Am I right?"

"Of course I was chasing a mouse," said Pussy. "And I still would be if I could get Tozer to move."

"You haven't found the mittens?" I asked.

"Of course I haven't found the mittens," she said.

My theory had been proved right.

But my other theory had been proved wrong. Or had it? Maybe Tozer really was lying on the mittens, and that was why he'd refused to move.

I stood directly in front of Tozer. My body certainly wasn't strong enough to move his, but I have a will of iron, and now I put all the power of my iron will into the order I gave him:

"Stand up, Tozer," I said. "Immediately."

"Go and cook yourself," he said.

It was an extremely rude thing to say, and I told him so. He didn't even have the courtesy to listen to me. He just closed his eyes and snored.

There was no doubt that he was guilty. I could even see the little bumps in his body where he was lying on top of the twelve mittens. But how could I move him? The answer came in the form of yet another idea:

"Listen," I whispered to the three kittens. "If you want your mittens, you'll have to get Tozer to move."

"How?" they whispered back.

"Any way you like," I said.

After all, they wanted the mittens, so why should I do all the work? They thought hard for a moment or two, and then the first kitten said:

"I know! We could bite Tozer's bottom."

"Ugh!" said the second kitten. "That won't taste very nice."

"I'd rather have Mummy's pie!" said the third kitten.

"It's the only way you'll *get* Mummy's pie," I said.

They knew that I was right. We all crept back to Tozer's corner, and when I gave them the signal, they pounced on Tozer and bit his bottom.

"Ow bow wow!" yelled Tozer, and leapt to his feet.

"Aha!" I said triumphantly.

But then, to my surprise, I saw that there were no mittens on the ground beneath Tozer. There was just ground.

"Aheugh!" I said. "Erm . . . ah . . . come along, kittens . . ."

I ran out of that barn like a mouse in front of a pussy, and the kittens came racing after me.

"Well, we bit him," said the first kitten.

"So where are our mittens?" asked the second kitten.

"And where's our pie?" asked the third kitten.

"Aha!" I said. "Now there may have been a slight misunderstanding about this . . ."

There was a sudden, very strange interruption. Out of the sky, right in front of my beak, there fell . . . a mitten.

"What's this?" I asked.

"It's a mitten," said the first kitten.

"It's *my* mitten!" said the second kitten.

"No, it's not. It's mine!" said the third kitten.

"It's mine!" said the first kitten.

But as they began to fight over it, another mitten fell from the sky. I looked up, and there, circling above me, was Spiffy the Sparrow.

"Well?" called Spiffy. "Is them the mittens or ain't they?"

"Yes!" I cried. "Where did you get them, Spiffy?"

"I told yer," he said. "I pinched 'em. Only yer wouldn't believe me."

He flew back and forth ten more times, and each time he dropped another mitten from the sky. At last all three of the kittens were wearing all four of their mittens, and off they ran, crying:

"Mummy, Mummy! We've found our mittens! Please can we have our pie?"

"So?" said Spiffy. "Am I or am I not a master criminal?"

"Yes, you are, Spiffy," I said.

"Yippee!" he cried. "Yahoo! Yeehah! Whoopee!"

Then he turned a somersault in the middle of the yard, flew into the air, did a loop-the-loop, landed back in the yard, and stood on his beak.

That almost concluded the Case of the Missing Mittens. When the kittens had had their pie, they came across the yard to thank me.

"We knew you'd find our mittens for us, Uncle Gideon," they said.

I knew I would, too. Gideon Gander always solves his cases.

"What we don't understand," said the first kitten, "is how you did it."

"How I did it?" I asked.

"You told us that if we moved Tozer," said the second kitten, "we'd get our mittens back."

"And our pie," said the third kitten.

"That's right," I said. "And you did get your mittens and your pie."

"But how?" asked the first kitten.

"How did moving Tozer make Spiffy bring the mittens?" asked the second kitten.

"Why did Spiffy bring the mittens when we moved Tozer?" asked the third kitten.

They were good questions. And I didn't know the answers.

"Aha!" I said. "Well . . . Do you know the meaning of the word DNAECRIAMEFN?"

"No," they said.

"Pity," I said. "Well, one day, when you're old enough, you'll know the meaning of DNAECRIAMEFN, and then you'll know why Spiffy brought the mittens when we moved Tozer. But now I've got to go and give Gary a honking lesson. Bye-bye, kittens."

"Bye-bye, Uncle Gideon," they cried, "and thank you!"

Sometimes it's not just the criminals that you have to outsmart.

Pickled Pepper

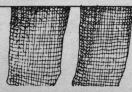

"Cold cross buns! Cold cross buns! One a penny, two a penny! Cold cross buns!"

The pieman regularly came to our farm, and we all enjoyed his buns, though I never quite understood his pricing system.

"It's quite simple, Mr Gideon," he said. "One a penny for the large ones, two a penny for the small ones. Now, which will it be?"

I bought the small ones. I'd worked it out that you could get twice as many small ones as large ones, so the small ones were obviously a better buy.

That was the start of a busy morning. The next visitor to the farm was Peter Piper. He'd picked a peck of pickled pepper, and was going around the district crying:

"Pickled pepper! Pickled pepper! A penny a pinch for Peter Piper's pickled pepper! Peter Piper's pickled pepper a penny a pinch!"

I bought a pinch of his pickled pepper, and away he went.

The next visitor was Simple Simon. He was selling nothing, and so he was going around the district crying:

"Nothing! Nothing! One a nothing, two a nothing! Nothing a pinch for my nothing!"

I asked him how much his nothing would cost, and he told me nothing, so I gave him nothing and got nothing in return.

I spent the rest of the day teaching Gary to eat his cold cross bun. I gave up in the end, and taught him to eat nothing instead. He found even that difficult.

I must confess that when I woke up the next day, I was hoping there would be a case for me to solve. One day of lessons with Gary is enough to get up any gander's dander. And so I was quite pleased when Peter Piper arrived at the farm, looking peeved, pained and pathetic.

"Someone's pinched my peck of pickled pepper!" he cried. "My peck of pickled pepper has been pinched."

"But who would want to pinch a peck of pickled pepper, Peter?" I asked.

"My pickled pepper's popular with plenty of people," said Peter. "Plenty of people are partial to my pickled pepper."

"When did you last see it?" I asked.

"I was passing Parson Pearson's parsonage," said Peter, "and popped in for a piece of Parson Pearson's pease pudding. I parked my peck of pickled pepper on the parsonage path, and some pilfering, pickpocketing pirate pinched it!"

"Don't worry, Peter," I said. "I'll find your peck of pickled pepper, I promise."

Promises are easy to make. They're not always so easy to keep. That peck of pickled pepper could be anywhere. I needed some more information.

"How was it packed?" I asked.

"I packed my pickled pepper in pepper pots and put the pepper pots in paper packets," said Peter.

"So if the thief wants the pickled pepper," I said, "he must take the pepper pots out of the paper."

There was only one thief, bold, ruthless and clever enough to go to Parson Pearson's parsonage, pinch the pepper, *and* take the pepper pots out of the paper packets. Wolfie! This was a Wolfie crime if ever I saw one.

"Allo, 'allo," said a familiar voice. "Somebody lost their mittens?"

It was Spiffy the Sparrow. I told him about the theft of the pickled pepper.

"Was it packed in pepper pots?" he asked.

"Yes," I said.

"An' was the pepper pots in paper packets?" he asked.

"Yes," I said.

"An' was the paper packets on Parson Pearson's path?" he asked.

105

"Yes, yes," I said.

"Sorry," he said, "I can't 'elp yer."

That was a disappointment. For a moment I'd thought Spiffy might be the thief.

"Don't yer wanner know 'ow I know?" asked Spiffy.

"How did you know?" I asked.

" 'Cos I over-'eard yer, didn't I?" said Spiffy. "I'd make a good detective, I would." And off he flew with a titter and a twitter.

At that moment we heard an unusual cry from the road:

"Hot cross buns! Hot cross buns! One a penny, two a penny, hot cross buns!"

"That's interesting," I said. "The pieman's got something new for us today."

And so he had. After he'd explained to me that the large ones were a penny each and the small ones were two a penny, he told us that he'd hit on a new recipe. From now on, he'd be selling *hot* cross buns. We tried them straight away, and it was Mother Goose who noticed the difference in the flavour.

"You've added pickled pepper," she said.

I congratulated the pieman. The pickled pepper made all the difference to the flavour, and I told him that if he carried on selling hot cross buns, I'd carry on eating them.

"Pickled pepper?" said Peter Piper.

"That's right," I said. "They're delicious. You should try one."

"Then the pieman pinched my peck of pickled pepper!" cried Peter.

Now, that hadn't occurred to me. To tell you the truth, I'd been so enjoying my hot cross bun that I'd completely forgotten about Peter Piper's peck. But once he'd spoken, I got straight back on the trail. In fact his words quickly led me to form a theory of my own:

"Pieman," I said, "you're a pickled-pepper-pincher!"

"No, I'm not," said the pieman.

That slightly spoilt my theory. Then Mother Goose asked him where he'd got his pickled pepper from, and he said he'd bought it.

"But you didn't buy it from Peter Piper, did you?" I cried.

"No," he said. "I bought it from Simple Simon."

"Aha!" I said. "I see. In that case, Peter, I think I've solved our mystery."

I was obviously a step ahead of everybody else, and so I explained to Peter Piper, the pieman, and Mother Goose exactly what had happened.

"Simple Simon stole the pickled pepper," I said, "and then he sold it to the pieman. The pickled-pepper-pincher is therefore Simple Simon."

It was a remarkable piece of detection. Now all we needed to do was find Simple Simon.

The next thing that happened was a strange coincidence. From the road came the sound of Simple Simon's voice, crying:

"Nothing! Nothing! Who'll give me nothing for my nothing?"

I was surprised that he even dared to come to the farm, but Simple Simon is not famous for his intelligence.

"We've got you, you pickled-pepper-pincher!" I cried. "You stole Peter Piper's peck of pickled pepper!"

His eyes opened wide, and his jaw opened wider.

"I didn't steal Piter Peeper's pick of peckled pipper!" he said.

"Didn't you?" I asked.

"No," he said. "I didn't."

And so the case had taken yet another unexpected turn. It seemed that every time I found the thief, he was not the thief after all. There was obviously something wrong somewhere, but I couldn't work out what it was. As luck would have it, Mother Goose then asked a question which was to put me back on the trail again:

"Didn't you sell some pickled pepper to the pieman?" she asked Simple Simon.

"Yes, I did," said Simple Simon.

"Aha!" I said. "So it *was* you . . ."

"Now, tell us," said Mother Goose, "where *you* got it from."

"I got it from Wolfie," said Simple Simon.

"Aha!" I cried. "Ahaaaa! I knew it. Wolfie's the thief! I've said so right from the start."

And so I had. Wolfie's name had been the very first that had come into my mind, and now I'd been proved right. It was a pity we'd had all these other distractions.

"Now then, Simple Simon," I said, "I want you to tell us exactly what happened."

Simple Simon explained that he had bumped into Wolfie the previous day, and Wolfie had asked him if he'd like to earn a whole lot of nothing. Simple Simon had said yes, and so Wolfie had given him several packets of pickled pepper. He'd told him to sell the pickled pepper to the pieman, bring the money back to Wolfie, and then Wolfie would give him as much nothing as he could carry.

"It was a good bargain," said Simple Simon. "Look at all the nothing I got."

"It seems to me," said the pieman, "that we'd better go and get the money back from Wolfie so that I can pay Peter Piper for the pickled pepper."

The pieman borrowed Farmer Green's shotgun, and then we all went together to Wolfie's place.

"Pickled pepper?" said Wolfie. "What pickled pepper?"

"The pickled pepper you pinched from Parson Pearson's parsonage path," cried Peter Piper, "and persuaded Pimple Pimon to purvey to the pieman to put in his pies and pastries!"

"Not me," said Wolfie. "You can't go round accusing innocent wolves like that, so you watch your Ps, if not your Qs."

"Stop bluffing, Wolfie," I said. "Simple Simon has told us all exactly what you did."

"Nobody ever believes Simple Simon," said Wolfie.

"I believe him," I said.

"Oh well, Goosey, you'd believe anything," said Wolfie.

He was deliberately insulting me. He knows I'm a gander, not a goose. But this time I had the perfect answer ready. I turned to the pieman.

"Shoot him," I said.

Wolfie hadn't expected that.

"Hold on, wait a minute, keep calm!" he cried, as the pieman raised the gun. "Don't fuss, don't panic, don't shoot! There's no need for violence. Besides, if you shoot me, you'll never get your money back."

That was true. I signalled to the pieman not to shoot. The pieman had already lowered the gun, anyway.

"Phew!" said Wolfie. "Pretty hot for the time of year."

"Stop stalling, Wolfie," I said. "I want this case settled."

"All right," said Wolfie, "a peck of pickled pepper, you say. And it's not easy to say, is it? I'll do my best. Pieman, how much did you pay Simple Simon for the peck of pickled pepper I'm supposed to have pinched from Peter Piper?"

"I paid him five pounds," said the pieman.

"Five pounds!" cried Wolfie. "Simple Simon, you only gave me four!"

"Maybe I'm not as simple as I look," said Simple Simon.

"Well, this is what I'm prepared to do," said Wolfie. "Out of the goodness of my heart, I will give Peter Piper two pounds of my own money, the pieman can give him two, and Simple Simon can give him one. Not that I'm admitting to anything, mind. I never stole a thing. I just want us all to live happily ever after. How about that, Goosey?"

"Gander!" I said.

"How about it, Goosey Gander?"

I'd found it all a little hard to follow, so I turned to the others.

"What do you think?" I asked.

"All right," said Peter Piper.

"All right," said Simple Simon.

"All wrong!" said the pieman. "I've already paid five pounds for the pickled pepper. Now I'm supposed

to pay seven, while Wolfie only pays two and keeps two of the four he got from me through Simple Simon."

"Exactly!" I said. "Just what I was thinking."

I was completely lost now, but the pieman obviously knew what he was talking about.

"Pieman," I said, "what do you think would be fair?"

"Wolfie must give four pounds to Peter Piper," said the pieman, "and Simple Simon must give one."

"That's a fair solution," I said, "and I'm in favour."

"But that means I get nothing for all my work!" said Wolfie.

"What work?" asked the pieman.

"What work?" I asked.

If the pieman wanted to know what work, then so did I. But Wolfie didn't answer. He probably hadn't done any work.

"All right," he said. "I agree."

Then Wolfie gave Peter Piper four pounds, Simple Simon gave him one pound, and we all had a hot cross bun to celebrate. I'd solved yet another mystery, and I'd got the better of Wolfie even if he hadn't confessed to his crime.

"One of these days," I said to him as we left, "I shall prove what a criminal you are."

"And in the meantime," said Wolfie, "I shall go on proving what a goose you are."

I suppose that was his idea of a joke.

The Missing Nose

"Come to the Palace immediately. The King wants to see you."

That was the message that started me off on one of my most famous cases. I can't say I was very keen to go back to the Palace. On my last visit, when I had solved the Humpty Dumpty Mystery, I'd had to dig up a grave, spend hours and hours reading toilet rolls in the Royal Lavatory, fill in the grave, and drag a heavy gravestone with egg-cup all the way to the river. And as a reward the King had wished me goodbye and good luck.

"Shall I tell him I can't come?" I asked Mother Goose.

"You can't say 'can't' to a King," she said. "Unless you want your head chopped off."

I decided to take the case.

"It's our maid," said the King. "She's lost her nose, and we've got to find it. If we don't, she won't do any more cooking, washing, cleaning or ironing. It's a national crisis. Find her nose, and there'll be a big reward for you."

The case sounded interesting. So did the reward.

"I'd better see her straight away," I said.

"You can't," said the King. "She's locked herself in the kitchen, and she won't come out till she gets her nose back."

"But I need to know what happened," I said.

"All I can tell you is that she was hanging the clothes out in the garden, screamed, and the next thing we knew was that she was locked in the kitchen without her nose."

"I see," I said.

I didn't see, but I had to say something.

"You can talk to her through the kitchen door if you like," said the King. "And by the way, you'd better try to avoid the Queen. She's in a foul temper because she can't get into the kitchen for her food."

The King showed me the way to the kitchen, stopping to peep round every corner in case the Queen was there. She wasn't.

"Probably sulking in the parlour," said the King. "This is the kitchen door."

"Hello, in there!" I called. "Can you hear me?"

"Of course I cad hear you," said a voice. "It's by dose I've lost, dot by ears!"

"This is Superdetective Gideon Gander of the Yard. I'm going to find your nose!"

"Thed what are you doig here? Go add fide it!"

"I need to know what happened," I said.

"I was haggig out the washig id the garded, add suddedly sobthig attacked be add took by dose. That's all I kdow."

"What attacked you?" I asked.

"I dote kdow."

"Think carefully," I said. "Was it a wolf?"

"Do," she said. "If it had beed a wolf, I'd have seed it."

That was a pity. If it wasn't Wolfie, I really didn't have much idea who it could be.

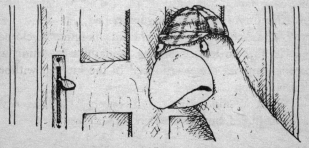

I asked the King to show me the garden where the maid had been hanging out the clothes. Fortunately, I didn't see the Queen, but what I did see when we reached the garden was a whole line of shirts, vests, pants, and fur-lined knickers. They looked suspicious.

"What are these?" I asked.

"Clothes," said the King.

"And what are they doing here?" I asked.

"The maid was hanging them out," said the King.

I quickly formed a theory. The clothes on the line could be the clothes the maid was hanging out when she was attacked. In other words, by sheer chance we were standing on or near the very spot where she had lost her nose.

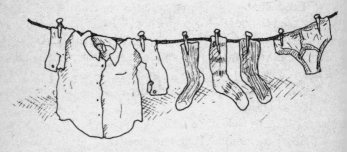

"It's my belief," I said to the King, "that this is the place where the nose was lost. Let's look for it."

"We have," said the King. "The gardener and I searched every inch of the garden."

"Aha!" I said. "And what did you find?"

"A few flowers," said the King, "and some vegetables, and a lot of weeds."

"Did you find a nose?" I asked.

"Of course we didn't find a nose!" said the King. "If we had, I wouldn't have sent for you!"

His tone was rather rude, but I didn't tell him so. He was probably upset at not having found the nose. Instead, I glanced around the garden and happened to see a black feather lying on the ground. I picked it up.

"Aha!" I said. "What's this?"

"It's a feather," said the King. "And if you ask me any more stupid questions, I shall have your head chopped off."

That was a shock. Rudeness is one thing, but head-chopping is quite another.

"You can't be serious, Your Majesty," I said.

"Just try me," he said.

I needed to impress him quickly. If only I could find a clue! If only I could see the nose!

"Well?" snapped the King. "Can you solve the case or can't you?"

"I think I've solved it already, Your Majesty," I said.

I was desperate.

"Where's the nose, then?" he asked.

"One step at a time, Your Majesty," I said. "The key to the mystery is . . . is . . . is this feather."

"What about the feather?" he asked.

"You'll soon see," I said.

Then I looked closely at the feather, shook it, listened to it, smelt it, tasted it, held it up in the wind . . .

"Well?" asked the King.

"Well . . ." I said. "Well, well."

"Well what?"

"Well, well, well."

"What have you found out?" he asked.

"Do you notice anything special about this feather, Your Majesty?" I asked him.

"No," he said.

That was a pity. I'd hoped he would. I certainly hadn't.

"Except that it's black," he said.

"Aha!" I said. "Precisely! And what does that mean?"

"I suppose it's fallen off a black bird."

That was quite good thinking. It might even be a clue, though I still didn't see what it had to do with the missing nose.

"Exactly," I said. "A black bird. The vital clue."

"So where's the nose?" asked the King.

"Just a few more questions, Your Majesty," I said, "and all will be revealed."

I was in terrible trouble. If all wasn't revealed, then, as far as I was concerned, all would be over. My only hope was to keep asking questions. Maybe the King would get tired, or hungry, or bored, and go away. Maybe the Queen would come and drag him off to the parlour.

"Where were you, Your Majesty, at the moment of the crime?"

"In the counting house," said the King.

"And where was the Queen?" I asked.

"In the parlour, eating bread and honey."

"And where was the gardener?"

"Washing up after lunch."

"And what did you have for lunch?"

"Blackbird pie."

"And what was in the blackbird pie?"

"Blackbirds, you silly goo . . . ah! Wait a moment!"

For some reason the King held up his hand. There was a look on his face which in a strange way reminded me of the dawn.

"Wait a moment!" he said again.

I waited. I was prepared to wait an hour so long as he didn't chop off my head.

"Blackbird pie . . ." he said. "Made with a pocketful of rye and twenty-four blackbirds. A very dainty dish it was, too. But I see what you're getting at."

I was glad that he did. I certainly didn't.

"In fact," he said, "something very interesting happened after we'd opened the pie."

"What was that, Your Majesty?" I asked.

"The birds began to sing," he said.

"The twenty-four blackbirds?" I asked.

"No," he said. "They'd been baked. It was the birds in the garden – they made a terrible din."

"That's very interesting," I said.

Actually, I thought it was rather boring, but you don't tell a King he's boring. Unless you want to lose your head.

"I remember thinking at the time," said the King, "that it was a protest. Blackbirds protesting about unfair treatment to blackbirds. It happens all the time. Usually it's people protesting about unfair treatment to people. It's a rotten life being a King. Everybody's always protesting about something. That's why I spend so much time in the counting house – it's the only place where I can get any peace."

"Tsk, tsk," I said. "Poor you."

"Well, this theory of yours could be right," said the King.

"What theory's that?" I asked.

"That a blackbird took the maid's nose as a protest."

"Exactly!" I said. "The blackbird did it!"

I didn't quite see how I'd reached that conclusion, but if the King thought I was right, then so did I.

"The problem is," said the King, "how do we get the nose back?"

He looked at me as though he expected an answer. I thought that was a bit unfair, since I didn't even know how the nose had been lost in the first place. But I remembered something my old mother had told me when I was just a tiny gosling:

"Maybe if you asked nicely . . ." I said.

"That's it!" cried the King. "I'll ask them to give it back, and I'll promise never to eat blackbird pie again."

"What a good idea, Your Majesty!" I said.

If he was happy with it, I was happy with it.

He hurried off to the counting house, and came back with a large sheet of paper and a pencil. Then, very slowly and carefully, he wrote out the following message:

PLEASE CAN WE HAVE OUR MAID'S
NOSE BACK
AND WE'LL NEVER EAT ANOTHER
BIRD THAT'S BLACK
signed, The King

Then he stuck it up on the Palace wall, and we waited.

We'd hardly waited for one minute when there was a flutter of black and a swoosh of pink, and there in front of us on the garden path lay a nose.

"We've done it!" cried the King. "We've got the nose back! Congratulations, Goose, my boy, you've saved the kingdom! I shall give you a knighthood for this. Wait here. I'll be back in a minute."

He rushed off, holding the nose, and I waited in the garden feeling rather pleased with myself. Mother Goose would have quite a surprise when she learned she was now married to Sir Gideon Gander. And it would be a shock for Wolfie, too. He'd have to show a bit more respect for me now that I was a knight. Maybe I'd have some visiting cards printed: Sir Gideon Gander, Superdetective. Then the whole town would know.

The King came back.

"Here you are, Goose," he said. "This is your reward, and well done again!"

He handed me a small piece of black cloth.

"Thank you, Your Majesty," I said. "What is it?"

"It's a nighthood," said the King. "You slip it over your head at night. Shuts out all the light and the noise, so you'll sleep better. The King of France gave it to me, but I couldn't breathe with it on, so you can have it. Goodbye, Goose, and good luck."

It wasn't the reward I'd expected, but when I showed it to Mother Goose, she said it was better to have a hood for my head than no head at all. And I could still tell everyone that the King had given me a knighthood, if I wanted to.

That night, I put the hood over my head and very nearly suffocated. I couldn't breathe with it on. If Mother Goose hadn't taken it off me in time, it would have been another case for investigation. But Sir Gideon Gander, Superdetective, would not have been there to solve it.

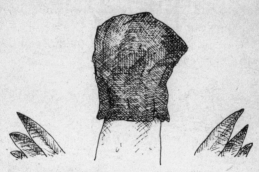

The End